Miss Davenport

The Field of Hum

Jon Gamble

Illustrations by Jennifer Black

Karuna Publishing

Published by Karuna Publishing
Yerrinbool, Australia 2019

Cataloguing-in-Publication details are available
from the National Library of Australia
www.librariesaustralia.nla.gov.au

ISBN 978-0-9752473-7-2

Book & Cover Design: Tina Mulholland
Illustrations by © Jennifer Black
Icon illustrations: Tina Mulholland
Cover Image: SJ Travel Photo and Video/Shutterstock

Printed in Australia.

This story is truly narrated & translated into Humenglish by your ever faithful witness,

Contents

Dramatis Personae

Ruby
young daughter of the Browns, who learns how to be a cat whisperer

Mr Fred Brown and Mrs Angela Brown
Ruby's parents

Bella
a girl at school given to bullying behaviour

Miss Milner
Ruby's school teacher

Darren
the Brown's casual farm labourer

Detective Sergeant Adams
a local policeman

The Taylors
neighbours of the Browns

The bearded man in the grey van
the animal hustler

The Mining Men

Dramatis Animalae

Penny
Ruby's cat, a fluffy, cream cat, who
learns how to be a human whisperer

Simone
Ruby's anxious, other cat, who has peculiar
'seeings'

Henrietta
a gluttonous sheep who is an expert
at getting through fences

Rufus
a fat ginger-haired old rat who thinks
mostly about himself and his belly

Marty
a helpful, grey marsupial mouse and personal
assistant to the Oracle

Miss Davenport
the very proper matriarch (boss) of the herd of five
sheep, who dislikes dirtiness and uncouth behaviour

The Oracle
a chubby, grey and white, silkie guinea pig,
with a white moustache, who appears to be
the repository of all wisdom, who has a problem
with borborygmus (wind at both ends)

I mind me in the days departed,
How often underneath the sun
With childish bounds I used to run
To a garden long deserted.

My childhood from my life is parted
My footsteps from the moss which drew
Its fairy circle 'round anew
The garden is deserted.

So hush! I will give you this leaf to keep,
See, I shut it inside your sweet cold hand
There, this is our secret! go to sleep,
You will wake and remember,
and understand.

Chapter 1

Ruby Makes a Curious Discovery Which is Not Met With Enthusiasm

The two cats could not tell what was in Ruby Brown's hand as she hurried down the garden path to wait at the gates for the school bus. Normally, Ruby just carried her school bag but today there was something *blue* in her other hand. Following Ruby as usual, their tails swinging like pendulums, Penny and Simone finally sat like sentinels at the farm gates, regarding Ruby as she turned to wave goodbye to her mother, who waved back from the front porch.

Henrietta, out in the field with the other sheep, spotted the hand-waving and decided to baaaahh loudly in the vain hope of a little hay for breakfast. Then Ollie, Ruby's guinea pig, sniffed the air at all the commotion, wondering if he should dart into his hutch to hide, or finish off *his* breakfast.

When the school bus arrived, none of the passengers noticed what Ruby was carrying as she stepped up and walked quietly along the aisle to the rear. People hardly ever

1

noticed Ruby. That's because she hardly every said anything and mostly kept to herself.

Ruby sat in her usual seat, her long auburn, pony tail swinging side to side just as her cats' tails had done. As usual, the other children had their earphones in and their noses in their devices - all except Ruby - who briefly glanced up from the big, old, blue poetry book on her lap to regard the forest of wired heads, which swayed to and fro in time to their music.

The two cats watched the bus as it vanished down the road. But just as they turned to walk back to the farmhouse, they noticed a grey van parked close to the paddock fence. In the van was a bearded man gazing out at *their* farm. They turned their backs on him, twitching their tails in irritation as they pranced back along the driveway.

Ruby had her nose in her book the entire trip to school. She had found the old book up in the attic amongst a stack of dusty boxes. Its cover, which was splitting open at its spine, said *Library of World Poetry, being Choice Selections from the Best Poets, edited by William Cullen Bryant.* When she first found it, she fingered the yellow pages, mottled with age, then put her nose on them to smell the paper. What a quaint, musty smell! Then she leafed through the pages, looking at all the old line-drawings. Now, when you read something on your Kindle, there is no smell at all, and you don't get any funny, old line-drawings. This book, although it was old, was actually *new to Ruby*, because it was *different*. Ruby had picked up the book and taken it down from the attic to show to her Mum, who said 'Yes, of course you can read it. I didn't even know it was up there.'

'Whose book is it?' asked Ruby.

Her mother, with flour all over her hands and busily kneading scone mix, simply shrugged.

'No idea, go ask your father, though I doubt it's his - he doesn't read poetry.'

It's funny how tiny decisions can lead to huge consequences. Although no one knew it yet. Ruby decided that she would read through *all 789* pages. And it was *tiny* writing too! Just as well she was a good reader! And whenever Ruby put her mind to do something, that's *precisely* what she did.

As she read through the poems, she didn't really understand all the words and some of them she would be sure to look up. But she liked the sound of the words, especially the really old ones which no one used any more, like *thou* and *thy*.

Some people love living in their imaginations. Ruby was one such person. And now that she had a book of old poetry, there were lots of new pictures for her to imagine.

The bus arrived at school and everyone funnelled out into the school yard. Still no one really noticed Ruby as she walked with her nose in her book. No one, that is, until she passed Bella, who often had something mean to say to Ruby.

'Oh my God, Ruby, what's that, a Bible? Don't tell me: you're now, like, a born again Christian!'

'No,' said Ruby, glancing up from the pages. 'It's a funny, old book of poems. I'll read one to you!'

'O.M.G. you have *got* to be joking. That's more boring than the *Bible*.'

'*Charmed magic casements*,' continued Ruby, not seeming to hear Bella's rebuke, '*opening on the foam of perilous seas in fairy lands forlorn*. Isn't *forlorn* a great word?'

Bella's jaw dropped and she shook her head in disbelief.

'Look Ruby, here's some good advice for you. *And* for everyone's sanity. Ditch the book! Get yourself, like, an *iPod* so you can listen to music like us *normal* people. Get yourself an iPhone - though who in their right mind would want to text *you* - God knows. Poetry is totally UNCOOL.'

'But I like it. Here, smell the paper,' she replied, holding the book up to Bella's face.

'Ruby! Hello Ruby…' Bella tapped her clenched fist with her open hand then held it to her mouth. 'Hello! Is this microphone working? Ruby Brown!' she said in a raised voice. 'NO ONE CARES ABOUT YOUR POETRY and old books like that are only useful if there is a shortage of toilet paper! Lose the book or lose what *few* friends you have! Which is probably none anyway.'

'You're wrong there. I have lots of friends. Though to be specific most of them are animals. And no need to worry about our toilet paper. Mum buys it in bulk. By the way,' Ruby studied Bella's fist, 'I don't think you can use your fist as a microphone. Unless there's something about human bio-electronics I don't know about.'

Bella sighed forcefully, 'OH MY GOD', shaking her head of red hair violently as she stomped off to talk to one of her friends.

Ruby wondered: 'How can Bella get so upset about one book? Quite bizarre!'

She looked at her own fist quizzically, wondering if there was indeed any way to use it as a microphone. She held it up to her mouth and made some musical sounds through her fist. 'Doooo do do doooo!' A few kids glanced at her briefly, shook their heads, then continued chatting. Ruby didn't mind. No one talked to her much at school anyway. She was used to it. Maybe she should ask her Mum for an iPhone? She pencilled a note about that for later.

The school bell rang and Ruby put her book away carefully, but as she was going inside, her classmates heard her mutter some strange words to herself: "Perilous seas in fairy lands forlorn".

Later that day, when it was time for Current News in class, Ruby put her hand up.

'I've found a poetry book from the olden days. It's quite a mystery, no one knows who owned it. I found it in our attic. I can read a bit of a poem.'

'Yes, Ruby,' said Miss Milner, a little surprised, as Ruby seldom volunteered anything in class. She mostly just kept quiet. 'Come and read a verse of your poem.'

An instantaneous moan came from the back of the class.

'That will do, thank you, Bella', snapped Miss Milner. 'Unless you have something of your own to offer?'

'No Miss.'

'Go ahead Ruby.'

'It's by Mr Keats', said Ruby, 'page 237':

The voice I hear this passing night was heard
In ancient days by emperor and clown:
Perhaps the self same song that found a path
Through the sad heart of Ruth, when, sick for home,
She stood in tears amid the alien corn;
The same that ofttimes hath
Charmed magic casements opening on the foam
of perilous seas in fairy lands forlorn.

'Thank you Ruby. Any comments class?'

There was nothing but a sullen silence. Although you could *almost* hear Bella at the back of the class rolling her eyes.

On the bus back home that day, Ruby turned a page of her treasured book to find a *mysterious* paper note, in old, frilly handwriting. It said:

Though my days are dark and I see no hope
out of my present circumstances, still,
I find great comfort within these pages.
I shall repeat to you how to turn your dark days into light.

Ruby made another note to ask her Mum what it meant, and who wrote it.

The bus stopped at her farm and she raced down the steps. Penny and Simone where in sentinel position at the gate to greet her, their tails twitching in expectation. Ruby noticed some wildflowers growing just by the fence and picked a few.

'I'll leave them here by the gate,' she said to the cats as she nestled them in a careful pattern on the ground. 'They'll be here when we come back in the morning.'

After Ruby and the cats had disappeared inside the house, a grey van drove up and parked by the gate, its wheels crushing Ruby's flower arrangement.

Chapter 2

A Clever Plan is Devised to Save Penny and Two Unlikely Characters Become Strangely Intimate

If you stood at the gate to Oat Hollow, just where the two cats always sit to watch Ruby catch the school bus, and looked into the farm, here is what you would see. Your eyes would entice you down a narrow drive, bordered on one side by a generous flower garden and on the other by one of the greenest fields that you will ever see. You might see a sheep or two in that field. At the end of the drive sat Ruby's house: a green weatherboard cottage which, although quite old, was well loved and cared for. It had two storeys, and it's new, iron roof was white, so on a sunny day it shimmered in brightness. You would also see a huge oak tree, as old as the house itself. Someone - no one could remember who - had especially planted it in that spot many years ago. Just to the left of Ruby's house, and beyond the oak tree, stood the barn. It too was an old building, full of the smell of oats and sheep dung. Its old weather boards frequently came loose, exposing little gaps through which the sunlight could peep.

On this morning, if you got down on your hands and knees and peeped through one of these gaps in the weatherboards, you would see Rufus, a large, fat rat, lying on his back, on a bed of old hay and sheep dung, as the mid morning sun gently pencilled its way through many of these very gaps. One paw rested behind his head, his bottom paws crossed over each other. He had found a smelly piece of rubbery, old pork rind in the garbage yesterday and was chewing it up into tiny pieces, sucking the dry, old juices out of it. Like all rats, he loved pork rind: the older and smellier, the better.

Into this scene of perfect tranquility, poked the little head of Marty, through one of the larger gaps.

'Rufus: we need you! QUICK! It's something terrible!'

Rufus casually removed a morsel from his mouth, languidly sniffing once again its delicious aroma, and placed it reverently on his distended belly, so he could watch it bobbing up and down as he spoke.

'Can't you see I'm working?' he snapped.

Marty glanced briefly around the barn. 'What work?'

'Well, someone has to work on this pork and that someone is *me*. You as a rat *should know that*.'

'I am not a rat,' said Marty indignantly, 'I am a marsupial mouse of the species *Antechinus stuartii*. You know I am. And we need you NOW! Penny is in danger!'

'Yeah, well she can wait. She's just a stinky, old cat. Why

should *I* rush around just for *her*? We're supposed to be enemies aren't we? Rats like you and me. We don't like cats.'

'I keep telling you, I am *not* a rat! They are going to take her away!' Marty was determined to get Rufus out of the barn. 'For ever! Think about it. That means there will be only *half* the amount of cat meat put out each day.'

'So what! There's plenty of garbage. It's far more fun diving for treasures in the garbage than finishing off old cat meat. You always find surprises in there.'

'Rufus! If they take away Penny they'll replace her with two, young, *male* cats. I heard Mr Brown say so. Young, male cats *love* catching rats!'

Rufus sat up; the pork rind tumbled off his belly onto the ground. His bushy brows pressed into a frown. 'I think you might have a point there.'

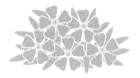

When Marty and Rufus arrived at the oak tree there was already an Assembly of Animals. All five sheep were present, neatly arranged in orderly rows by the matriarch sheep, Miss Davenport. Both cats were there, Penny and Simone, so were the two rabbits. There was an odd chicken or two pecking around but they were too absorbed in their grubs to notice the hubbub. It must have been really important if all the animals had come together.

Penny sharpened her claws on the oak tree.

Rufus and Marty sat beside the neat line of sheep.

Miss Davenport, sniffing the air near Rufus, howled: 'What is that ghastly smell?'

'Pork rind,' replied Rufus. 'Want some?'

'You know well enough that only clean creatures may attend our Assembly. We've all been waiting for you half the morning, and now you appear stinking of old meat! It's disgraceful!'

'Yeah, well I was forced to come. I have more important things to do. Just forget it: I'll go back to my work.'

'What work was that?' Miss Davenport was very prickly, rising to her feet. 'Hmmm? What work is more important than the life of our dear Penny? Didn't Marty tell you she is in danger?'

'Yeah! Well what can I do about it?'

'You can be quiet and listen! And let me tell you some-thing. If you ever come to one of our Assemblies smelling like that again, I'll box your ears. *Is that clear?*'

Rufus, a bit rattled, looked around his fellow animals for a glimmer of support, but everyone purposely looked away.

'Hmm Hmm,' he muttered quietly.

'Excuse me?' said Miss Davenport. 'I don't think we quite heard you.'

'Okay alright!' he shouted.

Having finished a satisfying claw scratch, Penny at last shook her head so her bell collar could be heard.

'Thank you Miss Davenport,' she said. 'Now ...' - Penny held out a beckoning paw to Marty, only to notice a spot she had missed this morning. Licking her paw quickly, she continued- 'I want Marty to come forward and tell us all what he heard. Marty!'

Little Marty stood up shakily, unused to being the centre of attention.

'I was out in the garden early this morning, under the box hedge, sniffing out bugs. Mr Brown was talking to Mrs Brown on the front verandah. I heard him very clearly. He said "Penny has to go. She serves no purpose on this farm. She just lies under that oak tree all day. I've never seen her catch a single rat, and the barn is full of them. *Every bag of my oats* has been chewed open again. The whole lot is spoiled. All my hard work down the drain. We need a *young, common moggie* cat that will go after rats. Penny is too old to be of any use on a farm!"

'Then Mrs Brown said "You know Ruby just loves that cat. She'd be very upset."

'"We can get her *two* new cats. *Young male cats* - and they'll catch rats!" and then he strode away angrily into the field.'

'Thank you Marty, good report. Now...' Penny briefly scrutinised her other paw to be sure there were no unwashed spots there too. 'Now, I am going to ask Simone to tell you about her *seeing*.'

'Oh, do you really think I should?' sighed Simone. 'I'm not good at public speaking you know.'

'I think it's important. Don't be frightened,' said Penny.

Don't be frightened,
oh no, no, no

A chorus of sheep rang out to encourage her.

Don't be frightened
Today today,
Don't be frightened today!

Following Penny's example, Simone quickly checked her own front paws to make sure they had been *completely* cleaned. And just to be sure, she gave the top of her tail a hurried lick. 'Well…I get these strange *seeings* sometimes,' she said, 'and … and … I *saw* that something terrible will happen to Penny, but I couldn't see what it was …' She burst into tears.

'Oh great! *Tears!* This is just *brilliant!* Rufus looked up to the heavens in the vague hope of divine intervention. 'There I was, seriously working on my pork rind,' he groaned, 'only to be dragged away for this …. Don't any of you think I have a life of my own? You think I should just drop everything and come running at a whim? Well, it's just too much!'

Miss Davenport stood up stiffly again and poked her snout right down into Rufus' face. 'It's not your turn to speak, you uncouth rodent! Quiet!'

Rufus swallowed. 'I don't even know what she means by *seeings*!' he complained.

'*Seeings*,' Penny took over, 'are just like dreams, except that sometimes they might come true.'

'Well why didn't she say so? My time is valuable, you know….' Rufus sat down and irritably scratched behind his ear as Miss Davenport fixed her eyes on him.

'Where are all these rats, Rufus? The ones Mr Brown is complaining about?'

Rufus felt like escaping but Miss Davenport had him nailed with her glare.

She continued: 'And why don't they have the good sense not to ruin all the oat bags?'

Everyone stared at Rufus for an answer. He glanced around the Assembly briefly.

'Okay it was me! Alright? Happy? There are no other rats, just me. It's alright for the rest of you. You all get fed. I don't! I have to scavenge. But *why don't we all just blame Rufus for everything!* If it makes you all feel better.'

Miss Davenport's continued her glare. 'All the oat bags? Every one of them? What were you thinking? I'll tell you what you were thinking. *You* were *only* thinking of yourself. You're fatter than all of us, so I won't hear any complaints about lack of food. And now look at the danger you have caused for Penny!'

'What are we going to do?' cried Simone. 'I couldn't bear it if Penny was taken. And what if they decide to get rid of me too?'

'I have a plan,' said Miss Davenport. 'It is not ideal! But I believe it will solve our problem. And it will require contribution from *you*, Rufus!'

'Me? Why do I always have to sort out everyone's mess?'

'Because YOU HAVE CREATED this mess,' snapped Miss Davenport.

*You created the mess,
oh me, oh my,
you created the mess!*

chorussed the other sheep.

'Now,' continued Miss Davenport, 'you will report here, *early* each morning. You will submit yourself to Penny. She will pick you up by the scruff of your grubby neck and parade you each day around the front garden. You will pretend you are caught and helpless and Mr Brown will change his mind about Penny. He'll be satisfied that she is doing her job of catching rats. *Is that clear?*' she chimed.

'What makes you think I am going to do that?' scoffed Rufus defiantly.

Miss Davenport thrust her face down directly against Rufus' twitching little nose, her breath a hot gale against him. 'Did you say something Rufus? I think I might have missed it?'

Rufus' beady, little eyes darted *urgently* from one animal to the next, searching for a glimmer of support from anyone. But even Marty just looked away. So, defeated, he just bowed his head and said, 'Yeah, alright. When does this charade start?'

'NOW,' croaked Miss Davenport. 'Now: have you at least washed behind your neck?'

Rufus considered his answer carefully. 'How recently do you mean?'

'Go and wash right now!' Miss Davenport snapped. 'Penny is not putting her mouth on a dirty scruff. Marty, you go with him and make sure he washes properly! Then come straight back here, otherwise I will personally come and get you, Rufus. And I can assure you that *won't be pretty!*'

Rufus swallowed uncomfortably at what "not being pretty" could imply and slinked away with Marty, paw in paw.

'Simone, dear,' said Penny. 'Now you *know* what your seeing was all about! And now you know that it won't come true! Miss Davenport has worked out how to fix things.'

'Yes, thank goodness,' Simone sighed thankfully.

When the rat and marsupial mouse returned, Miss Davenport sniffed Rufus over thoroughly, giving a cursory nod of approval.

Rufus, defeated, submitted himself to the beautiful Penny. 'Your Ladyship' was all he could utter, bowing his head.

This was not something Penny was familiar with. It was not something she *wanted* to be familiar with. But with dignity she applied her strong teeth to his scruffy neck and lifted him into the air.

'Start squealing!' Simone instructed '- so the humans will hear!'

'Grrh … Hmmmm … Grrrrhh' … Penny was trying to say something.

'Don't talk with your mouth full!' Rufus quipped, chuckling to himself.

Penny plonked him on the ground. 'Let's have a practice first, so we get it right,' she said. Then she sunk her teeth in him again and the troupe set off on its practice run. Penny dropped poor Rufus once or twice, and had to pick him up again. Rufus tried out some blood-curdling screams of agony and terror. His screams were so real that the sheep darted away in fright … until they remembered it was only pretending.

Meanwhile, back under the oak tree, Simone shivered as the wind changed direction and her heart sank as she saw dark clouds gather far away on the horizon. She didn't really feel as relieved as she felt she *ought* to.

Simone would not have slept peacefully that night if she had known what those dark clouds would bring, in just a few day's time. Nor did she notice the grey van hovering out on the road.

Chapter 3

Dark Clouds Arrive and Oat Hollow is Plunged Into Despair

Even in Winter, if it was a sunny morning, the Brown family enjoyed their breakfast out on the front verandah. From that vantage point Mr Brown surveyed his farm with satisfaction. Ruby could call out to her animal family, although her parents discouraged her from calling the sheep, because at the sound of Ruby calling, greedy Henrietta was prone to baaahing for more food, even though she had plenty.

And a curious thing: over the last week, Penny had been catching the pesty barn rats! Can you believe it! Just as the Browns sat down to breakfast, Penny would appear from the barn with a big, ugly rat in her mouth, and parade it around the garden, while the poor creature would squeal wildly, wriggling dramatically to escape its captor's vicious grip. Sometimes it would succeed: Penny would drop her prize catch and the rat would attempt to scamper away. Unfortunately, it was always a big, fat, slow rat. It could not run fast. Penny would scoop it up and triumphantly carry it away into the field somewhere, where it presumably met its demise.

Mr Brown was happy, because no more oat bags were being ruined.

Ruby was happy because her beloved cat would not have to be sent away in disgrace.

Mrs Brown was happy because her husband and Ruby were happy.

On this particular morning, as the family were settled on the verandah, Ruby noticed a grey van way out on the road, just outside their gate. It drove off just as her Mum brought out the coffee tray.

'Who was in that grey van, Dad?' she asked.

Mr Brown had his nose in the local paper. 'What's that? What van?' He stretched his head up over his paper and peered over the top of his reading glasses. 'I don't see any van?'

'It's gone now,' said Ruby.

He shrugged. 'Maybe they've downsized the school bus and you have just missed it?'

'I don't think they'd fit everyone into a van, Dad.'

Her father sighed quietly and smiled at Ruby gently. 'I was just making a little joke, my precious. I'm sure it's nothing.'

'It's time to brush your teeth and get your school bag, Ruby,' said her Mum.

'But we haven't seen Penny catch her rat! I can't go without seeing that!'

'Well maybe she's taking longer this morning. Hurry up now! You'll miss the bus!'

Ruby stood up to go inside. "Penny?' she called.

'Hurry up now,' repeated her mother.

Ruby strode down the garden path and along the drive to the gate. But only one cat followed her today. 'Mum!' she shouted back to the house. 'Where's Penny?'

Mrs Brown, waving goodbye from the verandah, thought it odd that Penny did not follow Ruby to the gate. Penny always did that, even in horrible weather.

'You go on!' she called back. 'I'll go find her! Have a lovely day!'

Ruby did not feel right. There was only one feline sentinel at the gate today. She knelt down to stroke Simone under the chin: 'Go find Penny!'

As the bus slowed down to stop, Ruby quickly placed some more wildflowers - in a different spot - where no one would drive over them, then stepped up onto the bus.

Simone wasted no time in searching for Penny. She sniffed around the oak tree: no fresh scent there. She inspected the flower garden, Penny's second favourite place. She ran into the barn. Rufus was there but no one else. She ran back into the house and up the stairs. No sign of her.

Suddenly she was reminded of her *seeing* of the previous week. No …no … no! That was all sorted out once Penny's started "catching" Rufus each day. Surely that was the end of that *seeing*? She miaowed loudly at Mrs Brown, who just brushed her aside as she busied about clearing away the breakfast dishes. Simone rocketed out to the sheep field and found Miss Davenport.

'Miss D…' Simone was quite breathless. 'Miss Davenport! Please come quick!'

'What is it my dear?' said Miss Davenport, raising her head from the pasture she was so enjoying. 'I do hope it's something important. You're disturbing my breakfast!'

Hearing the word "breakfast", Henrietta looked up briskly, her mouth full of grass.

'Penny is m...m...missing!' cried Simone.

'Missing? What do you mean, *missing*?'

'I can't find her *anywhere! I haven't seen her since breakfast!*'

Henrietta baaahed as she heard again her favourite word, breakfast. But in that instant, grey clouds on the horizon announced their potent arrival with cold, swirling winds. Simone felt her fur ruffled, adding to her chilled, unnerving feeling.

Miss Davenport greeted the news with some alarm: 'She may be lying somewhere sick or with a broken leg, or fallen down a hole!'

Fallen down a hole!
A hole, a hole!'

bleated the other sheep in unison,

Fallen down a hole!

they cried, kicking their legs up and jumping in circles,

Lying with a broken leg! a leg,
Lying with a broken leg!

'This is no time for hysteria!' scolded Miss Davenport. 'We must search for her immediately. Everyone go in pairs and Marty: you go and get Rufus, if you can find him.'

'I know where he'll be.' said Marty confidently.

One need not fully describe the scene that night when Ruby arrived home to find Penny was still missing. Of course

Ruby was in tears. She did not want her dinner. She did not want to go to bed: not without her Penny. But eventually, reluctantly, she allowed her Mum to put her to bed.

'Can I read you a poem from your book,' volunteered Ruby's Mum. 'Maybe that will help?'

Ruby nodded silently, her sad eyes red and watery.

'I'll just open the book at random and see which poem we find.'

Ruby nodded again.

'Oh look! There's a little note at this page!'

Ruby sat up at once to look at the note. It was a *different* note to the one she had found earlier, yet the same handwriting.

Mrs Brown read:

This poem takes the darkness out of my soul
and soothes my troubled mind

'What a curious thing!' she said, half to herself, half to Ruby.

'Who wrote that note, Mummy?' asked Ruby. 'I found another one but I don't know what it means.' She rummaged under her pillow and took out the other note. 'See!'

Mrs Brown read the other note.

'I really have no idea. I'll ask your father.'

'He won't know,' said Ruby. 'I asked him already. He doesn't know whose book it is.'

'Then it's a mystery. Will I read you the poem then?'

Ruby nodded, and listened intently.

Come to these scenes of peace,
Where, to rivers murmuring,
The sweet birds all summer will sing,
Where cares, toil and sadness cease!
Stranger, does thy heart deplore
Friends whom thou wilt see no more?
Does thy wounded spirit prove
Pangs of hopeless, severed love?
Thee the stream that gushes clear,
Thee the birds that carol near,
Shall soothe, as silent thou dost lie
And dream of their wild lullaby;
Come to bless these scenes of peace,
Where cares, toil and sadness cease.

'I like that poem. And I'm going to imagine in my thoughts and dreams that Penny comes back to us tomorrow,' said Ruby hopefully. 'I'm going to repeat in my head, *Scenes of peace, where cares, toil and sadness cease.*'

'I'll do the same, and let's see if we can make it come true', answered her mother, stroking Ruby's head.

Ruby nodded, as her Mum kissed her forehead fondly and put out the light.

Ruby snuggled up and stroked Simone, who made a little 'burrrh' sound. 'You too Simone. You imagine that Penny returns to us and see if we can make it come true.'

'Burrrrh' repeated Simone.

Chapter 4

One Crisis is Solved and Yet Another Appears

The next morning the gloomy sky and winds persisted. Penny was still missing and everyone remained miserable. Even Rufus. In a funny kind of way he missed the daily parade around the garden with Penny's teeth in his scruff. Not that he enjoyed teeth in his neck. But if you're the only rat on a farm it can be a little lonely. Now he felt more important. After all, *he* was the one saving Penny.

Ruby had woken up to find still *only* Simone on her bed, making little whimpering sighs in her sleep.

Her Mum came in and sat on the side of her bed, stroking Ruby's forehead.

'Mum, I had a strange dream. Not a scary dream. And not a sad dream. But a ... sort of *real* dream.'

Her mother smiled and nodded.

'There was a lady wearing a long, dark coat. She stood at the edge of the sea, one foot on some low rocks. She gazed

out over a grey, windy ocean. She had long black hair and it blew wildly. I couldn't see her face because she gazed way out to the horizon. You could see the grey sky kneeling down to touch the sea.'

Her mother listened intently. She thought to herself: Ruby is starting to sound like one of the poets in that book!

'Then she half turned her head', Ruby continued, 'and I could just see a little of her face. Then she spoke to me. I can remember all the words, just like she said them: *Be without fear, child. I am with you every day. And you are never alone. Trust in nature, not in your worrying thoughts, and you will see.*

Her mother didn't know quite what to say. How could Ruby remember such adult language?

'The funny thing was, I *know* this lady, even though I couldn't see her face. At first I thought she must be you. But no, she wasn't. But if she is with me every day, who else could she be. My Dad? No, she's not my Dad!'

'Maybe she is your angel?' was all Mrs Brown could think to say.

Mrs Brown decided to keep Ruby home from school. The weather was poor. She felt upset. Ruby was upset. The house felt empty without Penny.

After lunch the cold winds ceased and a bashful sun peeped through the thinning clouds.

Simone was sitting "Sphinx" style under the oak tree, trying not to think of anything in particular, busying herself with licking here and there, when suddenly she had one of her *seeings*. 'I have to tell someone!' she thought.

She rocketed out into the barnyard, bumping square into Rufus as he was dragging smelly artefacts along the ground.

'Rufus: I've had a *seeing*! Penny is back!'

'Oh that's wonderful,' he cried. His first thought was that now there would again be two cat bowls to clean out each day. But he decided not to share that thought, so he said 'Let's go and tell the others.'

They bustled together Marty, all five sheep, and the rabbits, and ran out into the field, straining their eyes into the distance … waiting, and looking, and waiting ….

But it was not until the sun was setting that Simone stood up, her nose jutting out to the horizon, sniffing the air, ears slightly pinned back, her tail giving way to tiny tremors of excitement: 'There she is!' she cried.

The group stood up, inching forward in hesitant enthusiasm. Suddenly a dim, distant object zig-zagged its way through the field. Yes! It was Penny!

Everyone ran out to greet her. Penny was panting furiously, her heart pounding, her eyes wide in fear.

'What happened? Where have you been?' blurted Simone.

'A horrible man grabbed me,' she gasped, trying to catch her breath, '… put me in his van. I only went out to see what he was up to. He put a net over me. Took me to his house. I had to wait for the right moment to escape.'

'Was it the man with the beard?' asked Simone.

Penny nodded, still catching her breath.

Ruby spied all the animals out there in the field and ran out of the house in a flurry of excitement. Bounding over the clumps of grass and thistles, she reached the little group and fell on the ground in relief, bundling precious Penny into her arms and stroking her with pleasure.

'Never never never disappear again. I'll make sure you don't!' cried Ruby.

Oat Hollow quickly returned to normality…well, as normal as Oat Hollow *could* ever be, I suppose. Mrs Brown called the police. They told her other people had lost animals too, so they were on the lookout for the thief.

But now everyone, humans and animals, was particularly cautious about *vans*. If there was an animal thief from the outside world, no one wanted him to come back. So only two days later, the sight of *two* grey vans driving through the gate had everyone on high alert. The animals watched as a man got out of each van and went up the the Brown house to disturb their pleasant breakfast on the verandah.

'Is that the man?' Simone asked anxiously?

'No, they are different men. I'll go and see what all this is about!' said Penny, sprinting to the front verandah.

Simone followed quickly: 'Be careful! I don't trust men in vans!'

Sheep, rat, marsupial mouse, rabbits and assorted chickens gathered around the oak tree warily watching the cats slink up to the front of the house yard. Were these men going to try to take someone else away? What was the paper they were handing Mr Brown at the front door? Why was Mr Brown shaking his head and shouting at the men? Finally the two men shrugged apologetically and went back to their vans and drove away.

When the two feline spies returned everyone was in a dither. The sheep were jumping about in circles.

Simone said: 'The two men gave Mr Brown a letter. He read it out to Mrs Brown. The letter said that the men have permission to dig some big holes in the ground. Looking for ... what was it again?' Simone turned to Penny.

'Something black out of the ground', said Penny. 'I'm not quite sure what it is. Anyway, Mr Brown was very upset. He shouted "Over my dead body. They are not going to dig up our farm. I won't have it!". I've never really seen him so upset, that's for sure.' Penny resisted the temptation to lick her paws in front of everyone, so she contented herself with a quick claw sharpen on the oak tree to relieve her growing tension.

'Yes, he was awfully upset. If Mr Brown is so upset, what are we to make of it? What should we do?' echoed Simone.

'Holes in the ground?' said Henrietta. 'That will ruin the grass. That won't do at all!'

'What will happen to the farm?' asked Simone, fighting back tears.

'We must consult the Oracle', said Marty.

The O-ra-cle,
the O-ra-cle,
we must consult the O-ra-cle

chanted the sheep, still twitching and jumping.

'The what?' asked Rufus in exasperation. 'What on earth does "The Oracle" mean? First it was "seeings" and now it's "Oracle".

There was a silence. Then Penny volunteered: 'An earlier time, before you came to live on this farm, we had another crisis. I won't go into it. The Oracle knew what to do. He always knows what to do.'

'Shall I go and request an audience with him?' volunteered Marty.

'No need!' squeaked a feeble, little voice at the rear of the assembly. 'The Oracle is here!'

A fat-bottomed, grey and white, silkie guinea pig, ambled slowly through the crowd, a carrot stick in one paw, with which he supported his rotund, old body. His tail hair was so long it draped along the ground like a wedding gown.

The other animals reverently made space for him, bowing their heads as he ambled past. The sheep took the opportunity for an impromptu nibble at the grass, while the chickens scratched away hopefully at the leaves under the oak tree.

Ruby whispered to Marty. 'Is this a joke?'

'Shhhh. No!' whispered Marty in return.

'*That* guinea pig is your wise one?'

Marty nodded.

'Great,' said Rufus, mostly to himself. 'First we have a cat with *seeings*. Then I'm carried around the yard each morning by another cat. And now we are going to listen to an old guinea pig!'

Miss Davenport glared at Rufus, who decided that silence might be a safer course.

Everyone was suddenly attentive as the wise Oracle went to speak: The guinea pig slowly opened his little mouth and said … 'Burrrrp! … Ah, that feels better! No more celery for me today.'

'Oracle' said Penny. 'Simone has been having *seeings*. I was taken away by a horrible man. And now men in vans want to dig up the farm. What are we to do? What's going on?'

'You have good cause to be worried, my dear,' the Oracle replied. 'I had hoped not to see it in my life time, but alas, the folly of the human activity has now come to Oat Hollow and we are in peril. That is why I am here.'

'What is the black stuff they want to dig out of the ground?' asked Simone, her worried blue eyes widening. 'I don't like anything black. It just frightens me.'

'It is called coal. We cannot permit them to do so. If they do, it will ruin the farm.'

'Why do humans want this coal stuff out of the ground?' asked Rufus. 'Can you eat it?'

'No, you can't eat it.'

'What *can* you do with it, then?'

'You burn it.'

'Burn it!' scoffed Rufus, in his usual ratty tone. 'What's the point of digging something up if you're just going to go and burn it? You might as well just leave it there. Why do humans need it?'

'They don't need it. They want it, or some of them do, but they don't need it. They just think that they need it. And we will have to show them that they don't really need it and that it's better left safely in the ground.'

'How can we do that Oracle?' asked Simone. 'Humans can't speak our Fauninglish[1].'

'No,' said Rufus. 'Humans are not smart, are they? We can understand *their* Humenglish language but they can't understand *ours*. There's no way we can convince them to leave it there!'

---

1 *Fauninglish = The universal language of the animal world*

'This is going to need some thought,' said the Oracle.

'Can we stop them?,' asked Simone, suddenly starting to worry about more *seeings* coming to her.

'I hope that we can. But …' the Oracle trailed off, a look of anguish on his face.

'Oracle, are you alright?' asked Penny.

'Marty, quick!' replied the Oracle.

'What is it Your Grace!'

'A flea behind my ear…quick! And don't call me *Your Grace*', he mumbled, slightly irritated.

Chapter 5

The Farm is Under Threat

Ruby heard her father pacing up and down, muttering to himself. He paced from the kitchen through to the lounge, then back to the kitchen again, making a track in the carpet like the sheep do in the grass, Ruby thought.

'Over my dead body' he kept saying, shaking his head. Finally he strode out to the back paddocks to work.

Other times Ruby heard him shouting down the phone at someone. Then he would bang the phone down and stride outside. He did a lot of shouting and striding during that week. And the worry lines on his face grew deeper each day.

'We must be able to do something - surely - it's *our* home after all,' said Mrs Brown.

'I had a long talk with our local member of parliament,' said Mr Brown as he paced. 'He said we only own what's *above* the ground. The government owns what's beneath the ground. And the government has given the mining company permission to explore our farm. Other farms in the Shire too. I just can't believe it. There's nothing we can do!'

'That's silly. How can we own only above the ground. And how will they get coal out without wrecking our farm?'

'You're right,' Mr Brown was definitely flattening out the carpet. 'It *is* silly. I can't believe it's happening. There's a meeting in the town hall this afternoon. Our neighbours are going. So let's go too.'

'Even Ruby?'

'Yes, Ruby needs to know what's happening. We can't keep her sheltered from the outside world. We will *all* … be *affected*.'

With that he stomped out the kitchen door and strode out into the field. He didn't want his wife to see the tears collecting in his eyes.

Ruby crept into the lounge and sat next to her mother on the sofa. 'Why is Dad so upset? That's what Bella gets like at school!'

'The mining men want to dig holes in the farm,' she sighed.

'They mustn't ruin our flower garden! It's not theirs! It's ours!'

'They have a letter which says they can come and make some holes,' Mrs Brown sighed in despair, her head in her hands.

'Well, I'm going to tell them they can't touch the flower garden!'

Her Mum smiled distractedly. She felt her world was changing.

'Mum! I won't let them ruin our farm!'

These words snapped Mrs Brown out of her distraction. She studied Ruby. Apart from Penny going missing, Ruby *never* got upset. But now there was a new spark in her eyes. A flash of determination, or presence, which she had not seen in Ruby before. What was happening to Ruby?

'We made Penny come back, didn't we?'

Her mother nodded.

'So, we can make the farm safe too!'

'You do that Ruby,' Mrs Brown heard herself say. 'You tell the men!'

The two cats sat in their sentinel positions at the farm gate as they watch the family car drive down the road and through the rolling hillside. Ruby waved at them through the back seat window. The cats watched the car slowly fade away, then surveyed the area for any unwanted vans.

The town hall was full of people. Most of them Ruby didn't know, but a few of them were mums and dads she had seen at school.

It was very noisy. People were shouting. Ruby had to put her hands over her ears.

The Browns sat next to Mr Taylor. He was their neighbour who often came over to the Browns to talk.

Mr Taylor stood up and pointed angrily to the men at the front and said: 'This Shire has the most fertile, arable farming land of any in the whole State! It's a crazy idea to dig it up for coal!'

Ruby pencilled a note to herself to look up what *arable* meant.

'We can get coal out without wrecking the land on top,' replied the man at the front of the hall.

'What about the coal dust? What if you go open cut?'

'We have no plans for open cut,' replied the man at the front. 'Please understand we only intend to do long haul mining. You won't even know what is happening under the ground. It will be invisible to you.'

'What about subsidence?' called out someone from the back. 'I've read about it. The ground cracks and moves. What if that happens under your house, ha? Your house will get wrecked!'

Ruby didn't understand very well. But she knew everyone was angry.

Then another man stood up. Sitting by his side was Bella and her mum.

Bella's dad said: 'Yeah! And what about when you wrecked the underground creek up at Bowman's Creek? Then they had no ground water to farm any more. And they had to all pack up and leave! You wrecked the farms and they had to move away!'

'We will assure you that every care will be taken,' replied the man. 'Ground water tables will be avoided. Subsidence will be minimal.'

'What can we do?' asked Mrs Brown of her husband, her hand holding his arm. 'Will *we* have to leave our farm too?'

Mr Brown's worry lines stood out as he shook his head, 'I don't know what we can do!' He didn't want to try and answer her second question.

Ruby regarded her parents. Actually, if you were watching her that day, she did not *regard* them. It's more like she looked right *through* them. There was only one person watching her and that was Bella. But Bella's mouth was the first to drop open as the room hushed and she saw Ruby stand up on her chair.

'Ruby! Get down!' whispered her mother in shock.

The mining man at the front of the hall looked at Ruby. She was looking at him. And yet, he thought, she was not looking *at* him. She was looking *through* him.

'Can I help you?' he asked, puzzled.

There was a silence and the mining man grew a little uneasy.

Then Ruby said these words: 'The touch of nature's art, harmonises from heart to heart.'

Another long silence followed. Then one person somewhere started to clap. They slowly, slowly, everyone in the hall was clapping.

People funnelled out of the hall, shaking their heads and muttering to each other. Ruby saw Bella again and waved. Today Bella was not wearing her usual frown. Instead she gave Ruby a puzzled look.

Chapter 6

The Animals Learn About the Field of Hum

Exactly seven days after his first appearance, the Oracle turned up once more at the Morning Assembly. Again the group of animals parted reverently as he ambled his way through to stand by the oak tree.

The animals inched forward expectantly to hear the wise one's words.

The Oracle slowly opened his mouth and paused. Everyone thought he might burp again, but no. He was thinking ....

'Can we save our farm, Oracle?' pleaded Simone.

'Ha?' the Oracle shook himself out of his reverie. 'This is a very bad situation, so I have given it lots of thought. Can we save our farm? The answer is this ... maybe.'

'Only *maybe*?' pleaded Simone.

The Oracle started munching on his carrot walking stick, thinking to himself. 'Well, *possibly* then, not maybe. But we

have work to do. And it won't be easy. And we all have to work together. Is there anyone here who is not prepared to help?'

Miss Davenport decided to give Rufus one of her stares, just to be sure, but Rufus remained quiet.

'Very well,' said the Oracle. 'I am glad you are all silent, because that is first thing we must learn!'

'Excuse me, Your Oracleness,' said Rufus, despite Miss Davenport's glare. 'How is *being silent* going to save this farm from getting dug up? Don't we have to *do* something? I'm going to go nibble the tyres of their vans and let all the air out. Then they can't drive them.'

'Your enthusiasm is noted and appreciated, Rufus. But I fear the problem is bigger than that.'

'How come?'

'What is about to happen to *our* farm is happening to *other* farms. The ground is being dug up. The fields are being ruined. There's less space for food to grow. The air gets all fouled up with nasty fumes and black dust. Arrrgh!!!' The guinea pig suddenly jerked his head.

'Are you alright Oracle?' asked Penny.

'Marty! Another flea. Ruby needs to change the straw in my hutch more often!'

Marty attended the Oracle's flea issue as everyone waited.

'As I was saying,' continued the Oracle, '… what was I saying?'

'About farms getting ruined,' Penny reminded.

'Ah yes. We have a lot to learn. First lesson is silence.'

Rufus rolled his eyes but dared not say anything with Miss Davenport's eyes fixed on him.

'When do we start, Oracle?' asked Penny, trying to be patient.

'Tonight, as soon as the sun drops behind the barn. No later. I can't be out too late, because Ruby locks my hutch door for the night.'

'Us too,' said Simone.

'And we sheep get locked in the barn', said Miss Davenport.

47

'Us too', said the rabbits.

'Carrrk, Carrrk-carrk,' chimed in the chickens.

There was excitement in the air as everyone assembled that fateful night by the oak tree. The sun was low behind the barn and already the moon had lifted over the horizon, its luminescence bouncing off the white roof of the house.

Everyone was keen to find out how being *silent* could possibly save the farm. It didn't make any sense!

'This lesson will not take long,' the Oracle instructed, standing up on his haunches so that he seemed more important, since you would hardly say that guinea pigs are *tall* animals. 'It is best taught in the evening, when the sounds of the world are finished for the day. Once you learn it at night, you will be able to do it in the daytime too. The important thing is that you do not listen to the *sounds of the world*. You must listen to the spaces *between* the sounds.'

'That sounds tricky!' said Marty, his mousy ears twitching in anticipation and anxiety.

'No. It is not tricky,' reassured the wise one. 'It is easy. The most important thing is to not *think* about it. Only listen while you listen.'

'*Only listen while we listen?*'

'Yes. Do nothing else, except listen!' said the Oracle.

He picked up his carrot stick for a quick nibble, then remembered he was about to deliver an important lesson which required 'not listening to the sounds of the world', so he changed his mind and put his appetite aside for the moment.

The sheep collectively shook their heads in confusion. *Don't listen to sounds of the world? Such gobbledegook!*

'Are we all here?' asked the Oracle.

Miss Davenport briefly surveyed the group and sighed in exasperation. 'Marty!'

'What is it?'

'Go find Rufus, be quick.'

Marty raced off only to return a moment later with a reluctant Rufus, something smelly in his mouth. Rufus was careful to avoid Miss Davenport's disapproving glare.

The Oracle smiled gently. 'Now everyone! Tell me all the things you can hear.'

It was a still, quiet dusk. Not a breath of wind. The early evening chill was descending, heralding the likelihood of a frost.

Penny's ears pricked up. 'I can hear just two things. Your voice. And the sheep chewing their cud.'

'Attention all sheep!' snapped the Oracle. ' Stop chewing and be silent. Now all of you: listen *more carefully*. Not to my voice. What else can you hear?'

Rufus started chewing on whatever was in his mouth.

'Rufus!' scolded the Oracle, holding up his carrot stick.

Rufus put his food on the ground and scowled.

Penny's ears pricked up even further. She frowned slightly. Then she stared off into space somewhere. *'There's nothing to hear.'*

'Precisely. Now, what does nothing sound like? Listen to the space *in the middle of your head,* between your ears.'

Middle of the head,
middle of the head,
oh me, oh my

whispered the sheep in unison, trying hard not to make any chewing noises.

Rufus rolled his beady eyes: 'I think *some* of those present here have *more space* in their heads than others!'

'Quiet Rufus!' commanded the Oracle.

Penny concentrated very hard. 'Oh! Now I see what you mean. There's a kind of ... *hum!*'

'Precisely,' smiled the Oracle. 'It is the precious sound

which lies between the sounds. Now see if you can hear the Hum *outside* your head?'

Penny frowned and concentrated really hard again. Then she smiled. 'Oh yes,' she said, twitching her tail. 'When you listen for it, it's everywhere!'

'Precisely. It is everywhere, in everything, around everything, above and below everything. Everything has the Hum.'

'But everything *seems* separate and different,' quizzed Penny. 'You are you. I am me.'

'Only *thinking* makes things separate. When you stop thinking, there is only the Hum everywhere.'

'It's quite nice really,' said Simone. 'When you know the Hum is everywhere it means you are never alone and you don't have to be frightened.'

The Oracle nodded: 'Yes, only thinking makes you frightened.'

'I wish I didn't get so frightened,' sighed Simone.

'Can the rest of you hear the Hum?' asked the Oracle.

'Oh yes,' chimed Miss Davenport. 'It's funny isn't it. When you point it out, it's something that's already there, we just don't take notice of it. It's nothing new at all.'

'No,' agreed the Oracle, 'it's nothing new at all. How about you Marty? Rufus?'

'Yes, I can hear it,' said Marty. 'Though I would call it a *hiss*, not a *hum*.'

'It is the same, no matter how you describe it. And you, Rufus?'

'Ah pooh,' Rufus replied, frustrated. 'I can smell the cooking from the Brown house. How can I concentrate on anything else when I can smell food? I need to go eat!'

'Yes,' said the Oracle, 'when there's something from the outside world stealing your attention, you can't hear the Hum. Perhaps try again after your belly is full.'

'How come we all have to learn this stuff, if you'll excuse me asking, your Honour,' asked Rufus.

'Because if all of us learn about the Hum, it will be easier for Penny to succeed,' replied the Oracle. 'And don't call me your Honour!'

'I gotta go eat. I'm out of here', said Rufus, and, before Miss Davenport could say anything, he snatched up his food off the ground and raced away.

'Me? *I have to succeed*?' asked Penny. 'There's something you want *me* to do?'

'Yes, you are the go-between from us animals to Ruby. It is through Ruby that we might save the farm.'

'Why me?' she asked, feeling both overwhelmed *and* honoured.

'You are close to Ruby. You sleep with her.'

'So does Simone!'

'You are the right choice, Penny. Tomorrow, come to my

hutch for a private consultation and I will explain all the more about it. Come tomorrow after Ruby goes to school.'

'I don't want to hurt Ruby. She is my friend.'

'You will not hurt Ruby. You will save Ruby.'

'Save her from what?'

'From many things. Come tomorrow and I will explain.'

'Yes Oracle.'

'Now here is your homework everyone. Marty, make sure Rufus does his too.'

Marty nodded obediently.

'Practise listening to the Hum as often as you can. The more you hear it, the easier it is for me to teach you the next part. We do not have the luxury of time. We don't want to lose our home. Practise hard, so we can save our farm.'

'Sorry! Sorry …' mumbled Rufus, as he returned with something smelly in his mouth. 'I don't get it. How can listening to *nothing* save our farm? It's nuts!'

Miss Davenport stood up and started in Rufus' direction. But the Oracle raised a paw.

'It is a fair question.'

Miss Davenport felt a little miffed, but sat down again.

'I have shown you all how to hear the Field of Hum. It is only the first step. There are more steps to come. If we do not succeed, all will be lost. And you, Rufus, will help us save our farm. I will show you.'

The animals parted as the Oracle waddled back to his hutch before lock up time.

'This had better be good,' muttered Rufus to himself. 'As if doing *nothing* can save the farm! This place is just getting weirder by the day!'

As if to confirm Rufus' appraisal of the situation, the sound of a sheep chorus echoed as he strolled away:

Save our farm, save our farm,
So we can save our farm, oh yes,
So we can save our farm

sheep ears and tails were fluttering in excitement…

The Field of Hum
The Field of Hum
So we can save our farm, oh yes,
so we can save our farm.

The two cats ambled back to the farm house for the night.

'It makes me feel a bit sad, hearing the sound of the Hum, I don't know why,' said Simone.

Penelope stopped and looked deep into Simone's eyes. 'No, it's beautiful. The most beautiful music I have ever heard.'

Chapter 7

Penny Has a Private Audience With the Oracle and Learns to Feel the Field of Hum

The two grey vans were again in front of the house yard as Penny left the house to head over to the guinea pig hutch. She noticed the same too men looking over large maps and muttering in low voices. As she approached the hutch, Marty intercepted her.

'I'll just collect the rest of the Oracle's celery from the garden along the way. He can get quite gruff you know, unless he gets his morning celery.'

Dragging a celery stalk behind him, Marty led Penny to the Oracle's hutch and stuck his head through the door, talking quietly to the occupant. Then he turned around to Penny and announced, 'The Oracle will now see you!'.

Penny entered to find the Oracle chiselling away noisily on his first celery stalk of the day. Ever helpful, Marty poked his head through the door to see if anything was needed.

'Close the door if you please,' said the Oracle. 'We don't want everyone to know. If the sheep find out they'll get completely hysterical. You know what they're like!'

'Know about what?' asked Penny, starting to feel a little uncomfortable.

'The end of the world, my dear.'

'Won't it just go on forever?'

'Oat Hollow is in danger from the folly of certain humans who want to dig it all up. And what we don't see is what happens outside Oat Hollow. Sadly, the same human folly exists everywhere. Humans want to dig up the earth. Then they fight over who gets the spoils. The result is there is always fighting amongst humans and the world just gets ruined.'

'Why don't they just leave it in the ground and then they won't have to fight over it?'

'Indeed, why don't they just leave it? We will have to show them the folly of digging it up. And the folly of getting all upset about it.'

'Are humans really that silly? I can't see our Ruby destroying the world! And her parents are good people, aren't they?'

The Oracle smiled at the mention of Ruby (he rarely smiled about anything). 'Most people are good at heart, it's true. It is the small group of *influential* and greedy people who are ruining the world, not because they want to, but because they have forgotten about nature.'

'What can we do about it?'

'Do you know the meaning of the word, *alchemy?*'

'Turning base metal into gold, or something like that? I'm sure it's in one of the poems in Ruby's book.'

'That is the common understanding, yes. But to explain it better, I want you think of something you don't like.'

Penny thought for a moment. 'I don't like the dark, even though I am a cat and cats are supposed to be nocturnal creatures, I still get scared if I'm alone at night.'

'And what would you need to do to transform the dark?'

'Nothing - it transforms itself into daytime. You just have to wait.'

'Precisely. In nature, everything *transforms itself.* Night into day. Caterpillar into butterfly. But what about something out of nature, something bad which does not transform itself into its opposite, and is stuck just being bad?'

'Well … I suppose you have to *help* it transform into something else.'

'Precisely. You can't always get rid of bad things, but you can *help to transform* them into good things. That, my dear, is alchemy,' the wise one proudly proclaimed.

'What do you want me to do?' Penny asked tentatively. 'And how will it save our farm. I don't understand.'

'I will teach you, and you then will teach Ruby.'

'But how can I teach Ruby? Humans don't speak Fauninglish[2].'

'Mind Meld,' said the Oracle. 'That is today's lesson.'

There was a sudden knock at the door.

'Yes? What is it? I said I didn't want to be disturbed!' snapped the Oracle.

Little Marty meekly poked his head in the door. 'There's a crowd out here. The sheep are worried about those men with the vans.'

Vaaaaaans!
Vaaaaaaans!
Baaaaaaah!

The sheep refrain was deafening.

'Tell them we have things in hand. And don't disturb us again!' growled the Oracle.

'Sorry your Grace.'

'Baaaah', echoed a subdued sheep chorus.

'It's so irritating when he calls me that!' he muttered to himself.

Penny ignored the interruption. 'You said last night about saving Ruby from many things?'

'Yes. Did you know that Ruby is ... how shall I say ... *special?*'

---

2 *Fauninglish = universal language of the animal world*

'Yes, she is very special to me.'

The Oracle smiled. 'No that's not *quite* what I mean. I mean she is a little *different* to other human girls.'

'Is she? I don't know any other human girls, so I really couldn't say.'

'How shall I put it? Although she is part of the human tribe, she is also *not* part of the human tribe. Do you see what I mean?'

Penny quickly licked her paw to give her time to ponder this, then shook her head.

'She has no other *human* friends. She only has friends from the animal world. You, Simone, all of us. But no *human* friends.'

'Oh? I'd never thought about that. I imagined she sees her human friends when she goes off to school.'

'Have you ever seen her bring a human friend home?'

'Well, now that you mention it, no!'

'The human tribe is deteriorating too, not just the physical world. Humans are being born who don't fit into their tribe. To not belong to your tribe is a terrible thing for anyone, whether they are human or animal. Imagine having no true friends. Imagine not really understanding what other animals are trying to tell you. And the number of humans who are outside their tribe is increasing.'

'But I like Ruby just the way she is. She is kind to us. She cares for us.'

'Of course. I wish all humans were gentle and kind like Ruby. These are good traits. Yet she is an outcast from her human tribe. That will be a source of great suffering for her when she is older.'

'Oh, poor, little girl.'

'Our Mind Meld will save Ruby. She will be transformed, like a caterpillar into a butterfly. She will rejoin her human tribe. And then she will *transform* others.'

'Mind … Meld? I don't understand?'

'I will teach you. We will start now. Marty!'

'Yes, Oh Great One?" replied Marty, his head poking through the door.

'Would you be so good as to bring me another celery? And then we don't want to be disturbed again until finished.'

'Yes, Your Greatness.'

'I wish he wouldn't call me Your Greatness', he sighed, this time to Penny.

A knock came at the door.

'Ah, Marty was quick!' said the Oracle. 'Enter!'

It was Rufus, not Marty, who poked his head in the door.

'Marty is shooing the sheep away. So I am bringing your celery,' said Rufus, handing it to the Oracle.

'Someone's eaten all the leaves off the top!' growled the Oracle.

'I just tidied it up a bit for you. Easier for you to eat, Magnificent One.'

The Oracle gave Rufus a *Miss Davenport style* glare.

An awkward silence followed.

'Right ...' said Rufus. 'I can see you're busy.' He turned to leave. 'Any unwanted food remnants lying around?'

The Oracle said nothing, but pointed to the door with his tidied up piece of celery.

Once the door was closed and the Oracle was happily chewing on the celery, he began: 'Here is your first lesson. First, as I said last night, you must stop *all thinking*. Every thought must be banished from your head. Imagine you are watching a mouse hole, waiting for a mouse to appear. You will be alert and ready, so that you can pounce as soon as that mouse appears. But if your mind is wandering off somewhere in a daydream, you'll miss catching the mouse. That is how you must be *now*.'

'Yes, I can do that. No thoughts - all switched off!'

'If you catch yourself thinking thoughts, just drop them straight away and return to *No Thoughts*. An easy way to do that is to listen to the sound of Hum. When you listen to the silent hum which lies *between* the sounds of the world, thoughts will then stay away.'

'Alright.'

'Now put your paw against mine.'

Penny thought this was a little odd, nonetheless, she gave it a hurried clean, then did as she was told.

'Now put your mind into your paw.'

'What?'

'Put all your attention into your paw *instead* of your head. Feel your paw on mine.'

'Oh! Yes I can do that.'

'What do you feel there?'

'The warmth of your paw under mine.'

'And what else?'

Penny concentrated. 'The place *between* your paw and mine, where we meet.'

'Very good, you are a quick learner. I knew you would be. Very attentive. Now: I want you to dissolve that place: feel it *melt*. Feel the warmth of your paw extending right through my paw.'

'How?' said Penny, feeling a little lost.

'Don't think about it: keep your mind in your paw. Be patient. Wait. Allow it to happen all by itself. Forget about the idea of solid things. Forget about the idea of separateness. Now melt and dissolve the barrier, like butter melting on a warm plate. Imagine your paw going all the way down into mine.'

After a few minutes, Penny gasped, 'Oh! I am in your paw. That's weird!'

'What does it feel like?'

'Warm … roomy! It's like opening a door to a sunny room.'

'Precisely.'

'Now what do I do?'

'Ask permission to be together with me.'

'Oh! Yes, alright, I ask permission.'

'Good! That is enough. Now you can go practise Mind Meld with our other animal friends. You will find it easy with them. They will be easy to teach. Humans will be more difficult.'

'Why is that?'

'Because *humans think too much*. They mistake their thoughts for who they are. They think their thoughts are real when they are not.'

'But why do you think I can do this? I am just one little cat!'

'You are already in the field of *human understanding*. You have always been in that field. In an earlier time, you were with Ruby's Romantic poets. Surely you remember?'

'I just thought I learned the poems from Ruby. She loves poems.'

'Did you learn from her? Or did she learn from you?'

'I'm not sure what you mean.'

'Never mind about all that. You are the right choice.

Besides, you sleep on Ruby's bed at night. You have access to her.'

'So does Simone.'

'You can teach Simone too. Once she learns this, she won't be so anxious.'

'I don't want to hurt Ruby. I love her. She is my friend.'

'Ruby will not be harmed. She will be enriched. Remember the meaning of alchemy.'

'Enriched?'

The Oracle looked at Penny steadily. 'Once a human opens the door into that sunny room, his life becomes enriched. Obstacles disappear. Fear goes away.'

The Oracle let out a big burp, and rubbed his tummy. 'I think that will be plenty for your first lesson. Go and practise. Teach the other animals. Marty!'

'Yes Your Greatness?'

'Penny is leaving. And I am going to have a rest!'

As Penny was going through the door, she paused and turned to the Oracle, 'Your Greatness?' she quizzed. 'Why does he call you that?'

The Oracle shrugged. 'I am blessed to have such a loyal helper, even if he is somewhat over enthusiastic.'

That night, as Ruby drifted off to sleep, Penny gazed at the big blue book of poetry lying open on the end of Ruby's bed. She examined the picture, and looked at all the words. Then she nestled down beside Ruby. Simone was settled in on the other side. Ruby loved to be sandwiched between the two cats when she slept. Penny placed one front paw on Ruby's hand and practised exactly what the Oracle had taught her.

Chapter 8

The Animals are Discovered in a Peculiar Situation

'Mum!' cried Ruby urgently, running into the house from the chicken coop, a basket of fresh eggs on her arm.

'I'm in the kitchen,' called back Mrs Brown.

'Come and see the animals - quick - it's *amazing*!'

Thinking there must be an injury, or some other drama, Mrs Brown interrupted her breakfast preparations and followed Ruby outside.

What was *not* unusual was that the sheep, two cats, a rat, a marsupial mouse, a rabbit or two and a small gathering of chickens were nestled under the oak tree. What *was* unusual was that they appeared to be *holding* each other. Sheep paw against sheep paw. Cat paw against cat paw. Yet nothing else! All was still! No chewing of cud! No swishing of tails or twitching of ears! No scampering looking for bugs! No nibbling of grass! Only total stillness!

'Go and call your father,' said Ruby's mum, 'I've never seen anything like it.'

Ruby scampered out the kitchen door and called her father in the work shed: 'You must come quick, Dad, you have to see this!'

When Mr Brown saw the animal phenomenon from the verandah, he pushed his hat way back and scratched his head. 'What's going on? What's happened?.'

'What do you think they are doing,' asked Mrs Brown. 'Is there something wrong, do you think?'

'I don't know, to be sure. But I'm sure going to take a photo so I can show it to our Vet. Then I'll go and see what it's all about.'

Mr Brown checked his sheep, the rabbits, the chickens, Ruby's cats. He examined their paws for thistles. He looked at their eyes, their tongues, felt under their necks for any swelling. Nothing abnormal!

Next morning, as the family had breakfast on the verandah, again the animals were sitting in their little circle, under the oak tree, holding each other in silence. Darren, their casual farm hand, had joined them for breakfast today. When he saw the strange phenomenon he too pushed his hat far back, as he scratched his forehead and said: 'I never seen nothin' like *that*!'

And each morning, after the silent circle, Penny paraded proudly around the garden with a rat in her mouth, greeted by applause from the people viewing the performance. Then, with Rufus all the while squealing and waving his limbs in mock terror, Penny carried him, now emitting a deep, low growl, to the front of the barn, where Darren was to be found, scratching his head and muttering to himself. Finally she quietly released her "captive" and returned to the oak tree, where everyone then dispersed for their daily routines.

Somehow, word spread around the town about the behaviour of the animals at Oat Hollow, and a lady from the newspaper came out and took a photo. There it was on page 3 of the following week's *Wingaroo Post:*

Charming Circle of Animals – But Why?

Letters were subsequently written to the paper. One theory was that the animals had eaten weed poison, so were behaving strangely. But Mr Brown did not allow any poison on Oat Hollow. Another was that magic mushrooms were to blame, since if you eat them they can make you do strange things. Someone else wrote that the circle of animals could be linked to the mysterious crop circles that suddenly appear at random places all over the globe, whose cause is equally unknown and mysterious.

To dispel these theories, Mr Brown summoned his Veterinary physician to examine his animals. The Vet came and checked the animals, in much the same way as had Mr Brown, but shook his head and shrugged his shoulders. The Vet declared all were fit and healthy. When Mr Brown showed the photograph of the animals in their circle, the Vet said, 'I've never seen anything like that, and I doubt I ever will again!' Of course, that was a diagnosis already made by others.

The days rolled by. Mr Brown nodded approvingly each morning as he watched Penny with yet another rat in her jaws. You could almost discern the hint of a smile on his weather-worn face. Which was a nice change from the worried frown he was wearing lately. Darren continued his morning ritual, hat perched way back, surprising no one by muttering: 'I never seen nothin' like it!'

Penny's new morning routine never varied: Collect Rufus at the conclusion of morning Assembly which now included the Mind Meld practise with everyone.

'Is it my imagination, or are all those rats pretty much the same size?' asked Mr Brown. If he had any suspicion of what was really going on, he did not betray it.

'No, I'm sure not, dear,' is all Mrs Brown said, and that was the end of that.

Chapter 9

Ruby Astonishes Her Teacher

'Today, for English, we are going to take a look at the Romantic poets. Can anyone tell me why these poets are called *Romantic*?'

A boy put his hand up, 'Because two poets have fallen in love with each other, Miss?'

'Yes, it might sound like that, but no, that's not quite right.'

Ruby put her hand up.

'Ruby?' Miss Milner was surprised. 'What can you tell us?'

'The Romantic poets were in the 19th century. They wrote about capturing your feelings from your heart and translating them into words. And they looked to nature for their inspiration because they believed all the solutions to all the troubles of the world could be found in nature.'

Miss Milner was silent for a moment. 'How did you know all that, Ruby? Has somebody taught you all about poetry?'

'No, Miss. I've just been reading my big, blue book of poems.'

'Have you got your book here today?'

'Yes Miss.'

'Could I have a look at it please?'

Ruby carefully pulled out the big blue poetry book from her bag and handed it to her teacher.

'I'm reading through the whole book,' said Ruby, 'but I haven't finished yet.'

'I'm going to read a poem out to the class from your book,' said Miss Milner. 'Now let's see. Oh, here's a nice one:

Away, away from men and towns...

'Oh Yes! I know that one, it's lovely!' said Ruby.

'You know this one? Would *you* like to read it for us, Ruby?' Miss Milner passed the book back to Ruby. Normally, Ruby was quiet in class, so her teacher wanted to take advantage of this sudden change.

'It's alright, Miss, I know this one without the book.'

'You know it off by heart?"

'Yes, Miss.'

Impressed, Miss Milner contemplated Ruby in silence again. 'Please recite it, Ruby.'

Ruby stood up:

Away, away, from men and towns,
To the wild wood and the downs, –
To the silent wilderness
Where the soul need not repress
Its music, lest it should not find
An echo in another's mind
Where the touch of nature's art
Harmonises from heart to heart.

'That's astounding, Ruby, that you can remember all that by heart. Can anyone tell us what it means?'

'Someone's going off hiding in the forest, Miss,' called out the boy in front of Ruby.

'Yes. Why do you suppose they are going off into the forest?'

'So they won't get caught smoking at home?' volunteered Bella from the back of the class, which caused the other children to snicker.

'Is that what you do, Bella?' asked Miss Milner.

'No Miss.'

'Does anyone else have anything to say about this poem?'

Ruby was the only one who put her hand up.

'Yes Ruby.'

'It's a poem by Mr Shelley. He goes to the forest, not to smoke, although he might have done so while he was there (more snickering from the class). He's saying that when you are around other people, you have to keep parts of yourself hidden, because other people will make judgements about you. In the forest, there is only nature, and there is no one to judge you. You can just be yourself. But even more than that, he feels more connected to people when he is in the beauty of nature. But in the company of others, he feels too different. He is lonely when he's around other people.'

Stunned, Miss Milner, had no idea what to say. 'Um… did you read that in this book, Ruby?'

'No, Miss. I worked it out from the poem.'

Out in the school yard at lunch, Bella came up to Ruby as she was quietly reading her big, blue poetry book.

'Now you're, like, not just totally uncool, you're a freak as well! Congratulations!'

'Really?' said Ruby, glancing up from her book. 'How come?'

'No one likes freaks. And no one likes a teacher's pet, who's always showing off in front of the class. And what was all that about in the town hall the other day? You've so lost the plot!'

'I wonder why you get *so* upset about such little things, Bella? Is there trouble at home, maybe?'

Bella's mouth dropped open in disbelief. 'WHAT DID YOU SAY?'

'I presume you heard me, Bella, I was speaking at precisely the same volume. Are you being rhetorical?'

'Rhet… what? Look, don't you EVER EVER say anything about my home again! Not to anyone! *Is that clear?*'

'Very clear, Bella, no need to shout. Just trying to be helpful.'

Bella glanced around the school yard to see if anyone could have heard the conversation, then stormed off, muttering under her breath: 'Oh my God! Oh my God ….'

Maybe she doesn't know what *rhetorical* means, thought Ruby. Then she thought, well even though Bella always seems so upset about everything, she's the only other person at school who comes to talk to me. I suppose that's something.

That afternoon, shortly before the school bus returned Ruby home to Oat Hollow, Mrs Brown received a phone call.

'It's Miss Milner, Ruby's Year teacher.'

'Yes, Miss Milner. Is Ruby needing special help?'

'No! Quite the opposite, *I think*. May I ask you if Ruby has been having home tuition or something like that?'

'Tuition? No, not at all. Does she need tuition? I'm not sure we can afford it if she does.'

'Well no. It's incredible. Something has massively changed in Ruby. She's come out of her shell! She has always been good at her maths and science. But I didn't ever think that she understood the subtleties, and complexities, of *literature*. She's usually in a world of her own. But now she understands about ... well ... *feelings*. We did poetry today and she explained it all with a maturity far beyond her age ... I still can't believe it! There must be something that you're doing at home. Something different? Are you taking her to see someone ... professionally?'

'No! Goodness... I can't think what's happened. Except she found that old poetry book in the attic. She insists on taking it to school every day. I wondered if it would be a distraction from her school work, but then I thought - well - it's only a book of poems.'

'I can't explain it either. And that poetry book is really too old for her. Yet somehow she understands it.'

'Well, this is good, isn't it?' asked Mrs Brown.

'Yes, it's very good. But I'm worried it might alienate Ruby *even more* from the other children. They looked at her very strangely in class today. We just have to take care of Ruby's - you know - her emotional life. Even though she doesn't seem to mind what the other children think - and that's what worries me the most.'

'Oh yes', sighed Mrs Brown. 'We worry about that too - constantly. Ruby never gets invited to anything by the other school kids. And no one ever comes over here to play with her. And yet she seems very happy at home ... *perfectly* happy in fact. The only upset she's had recently was when one of her cats was stolen. But that's over now and everything is fine. Oh yes, and we have all the worry about the mining company. We're all worried. Especially my husband. And Ruby must hear him shouting down the phone.'

'Nothing *bad* is happening to Ruby, it's really *good*. I still can't believe it. You should be happy, actually.'

'Thank you. Yes, we are happy. Really!'

Chapter 10

The Sudden Appearance of a Cat Whisperer

It was at breakfast, one Tuesday morning, when the phenomenon was first noticed. Curiously, it was a breakfast like any other, a Tuesday like any other. Ruby was running late for the school bus like any other day, largely because she kept reading her poetry book at breakfast and lost track of time.

Yet Mrs Brown remembered for her whole life the very first time it happened.

Ruby was just finishing her egg when her mother asked: 'What do you want in your lunch today?'

Scarcely lifting her head from her book, Ruby replied, 'Miaow, miaow.'

Her mother turned her head to see what the cat wanted, only to find that there were no cats in the room that morning.

'What did you say?' asked her mother again.

'Miaow, miaow', repeated Ruby.

'What do you mean?' she asked.

'Sauerkraut and ham please', said Ruby.

Of course her mother thought nothing more of it, at least not for now. She must have misheard Ruby. Breakfast on school days can be frenetic, she had merely misheard her. That was it!

The following morning, Mrs Brown was ferreting around in the pantry when she heard Ruby talking to someone. Assuming that her husband had come in from the fields in search of his breakfast, she went back out to the kitchen. No husband! Only Ruby and the cats.

'Who were you talking to, Ruby?'

Ruby had just shovelled a big piece of pancake into her mouth, so her answer was delayed. 'Penny'.

'Right. Well tell Penny that you have to hurry up or you'll miss the bus!'

'I don't need to tell her Mummy, she understands you.'

'Then she will understand that you must not miss the bus, isn't that right, Penny?'

Penny blinked once at Mrs Brown.

Mrs Brown went back into the pantry, trying to remember what it was she was looking for, when she heard more conversation. This time she listened carefully. It sounded like a *real* conversation. Ruby would say something, then

Penny would respond 'Brrrrh, brrrr', then Ruby would say something else.

Coming out of the pantry, she studied her daughter. 'What is Penny saying?'

'She's telling me about the horrible man with the beard, the one who stole her.'

Her mother put her hand up to her throat and swallowed. 'Ruby, did you see the man who took Penny?'

'No. Penny told me what he looks like.'

'Why don't you ask her if she remembers the number plate of the man's van?'

Before Ruby said anything, Penny went 'Brrrh, brrrh, brrrh, shook her head, and blinked her eyes twice.

'Penny said it was "A Z Z 6 2 1",' said Ruby, then went on with her breakfast.

Before Mrs Brown could say anything, the door opened and her husband came in. Mr Brown had a look of proud satisfaction as he entered the kitchen and took off his hat.

'Ha! I've finally worked out where Henrietta is getting through the fence and into the house yard. She is the most obstinate of all the sheep, by far. So that's all fixed and now we won't have any more sheep demolishing the kitchen garden, and ...' he trailed off as he noticed the ashen look on his wife's face. 'What's the matter? Have you seen a ghost?'

How was she going to explain this to her husband? What would he think?

'Ruby knows the number plate of the man who stole Penny,' she said.

'What?' He looked at his daughter quizzically. 'How do you know that, my sweet?'

'Penny told me.'

Mr Brown's first instinct, as you would expect from most grown ups, was to brush the whole thing aside. But given the strange events which had occurred at Oat Hollow these last weeks, he held his tongue, searching for the right thing to say. But in the end he did not have to say anything: someone else spoke first.

'Baaaah!' came a voice outside the kitchen window.

'Oh for goodness sake,' yelled Mr Brown in exasperation. 'How did Henrietta get into the house yard? How many times do I have to fix the fence!'

To fully appreciate the profundity of the situation an explanation is needed. Henrietta spent all her days thinking about food. One day she decided that the tasty things growing in the kitchen garden looked more appealing than what was on offer in the field. So her daily challenge was to find a way through the fence. However, the problem with being by yourself if you are a sheep, is that you are frightened when you are alone: you only feel truly safe when you are with the herd. So, once she was in the house yard, Henrietta spent all day feeling distressed and tried to find a way back into the field to rejoin the herd. More recently, she just found it easier to 'Baaaah' incessantly at Mr Brown, so he would come and open the gate for her.

'I am going to call the police and tell them the number plate of that man's van. They have to catch him,' said Mrs Brown.

Mr Brown, distracted by Henrietta's calls, put his hat back on and reached for the door.

'For Goodness sake, they'll just think you're loopy. Don't do it!' And he was out the door and gone.

Maybe she was a bit loopy, maybe she wasn't. In any case, a strong feeling within, urged Mrs Brown to go and phone the police.

The Sergeant on the phone was a pleasant man, but to the point.

'You must have seen the man's vehicle when he drove off with your cat, Madam? Why didn't you report it earlier?'

'Well, actually no, it wasn't me,' she replied truthfully.

'Then excuse me for asking: how do you know the plate number?'

'My daughter told me.'

'Oh! So your *daughter* saw the vehicle's plate?'

'Not exactly "saw". More like "was told"'.

'Can I ask, who told your daughter, Mrs Brown? That person is the one I need to speak to.'

Mrs Brown hesitated. She didn't know what to say. But she didn't want to tell a lie either. And she didn't want the Sergeant to think she was loopy. But just as she was wondering what to say, Penny leapt off the chair, jumped up onto the phone table and stood up on her hind paws, resting her front paws against Mrs Brown and cried 'Miaow'.

'Umm … *that* was who saw the van', replied Mrs Brown, before she could stop herself.

'Your cat, Madam?'

'My *daughter's* cat, to be precise. My daughter's cat told her. And her cat saw the vehicle because she was the same cat who was stolen by that horrible man with the beard.'

There was a pause, quite a long pause, on the other end of the phone. Mrs Brown waited for the Sergeant to say something. She thought maybe she could hear him sighing. She didn't know what else to say.

Finally he said: 'You are telling me the thief has a beard? You are also telling me your daughter is a *cat whisperer*? Is that what you're saying, Mrs Brown?'

'Well … yes, I suppose I must be. Look, I don't pretend to understand it. But I know my daughter. I know the cats. I assure you my daughter does not make things up. And she does not tell lies. She doesn't even know *how* to tell lies. Even if you think it's odd, and it is odd I agree, what harm is there in simply looking up this number plate and seeing what you find? It's not the only odd thing happening on our farm. We are the people whose animals sit silently each morning in a circle!'

'You are the "animal circle" farm? The one in the paper?'

'Yes, that's us. So you see, when odd things happen, it's not so surprising for us any more.'

'Alright, as you say, there is no harm in running a number plate search', he replied, and Mrs Brown thought he sounded a little miffed. 'It only takes a minute. I *will* do it. Then I will let you know what I find. Good day Mrs Brown.'

And with that, he rang off.

Mrs Brown thought to herself: Well, that's the end of that! He'll just throw away the note and go about his business. My husband was right, he'll just think I'm loopy.

Two days went by. In the bustle of the farm, the ongoing battles with Henrietta, and going to school, and their mining worries, everyone forgot all about calling up the police. In fact, Mrs Brown didn't even bother to tell her husband about the conversation.

But then there was a phone call.

'Mrs Brown? This is Detective Sergeant Adams. We spoke earlier in the week about the animal hustler who stole your cat?'

'Oh! It's you! I thought you might have thought I was completely crazy and never given me the time of day. I've been embarrassed about calling you!'

'To be honest with you, that was my initial reaction. But I kept my promise and ran a check on that vehicle. I've located the van owner's house. It is a place out on the Old South Road, not that far from your farm, actually. So I paid a call out there and found many other stolen animals, including two King Charles Cavalier dogs, a prize breeding ram, a budgerigar, amongst others. Your daughter ... or I should say, your *cat*, was right.'

'Oh my goodness! Oh my goodness! I don't know what

to say! That's wonderful, of course, that you have found all those missing animals. But I have to tell you it's very, very weird when your daughter suddenly starts understanding her cat. What am I to do? We're just ordinary people, really. People will think we've gone mad!'

There was another long pause on the other end of the phone. Finally DS Adams said quietly, 'I have a small favour to ask of you, if you don't mind.'

'Hmm? Oh yes of course. I'm sure I owe you a favour after you took me seriously when you really had no reason to.'

'Could I bring my cat out to your farm? She's gone off her food and my wife is beside herself with worry. Our Vet can't find anything wrong. Maybe your daughter can find out?'

'Oh? Well I suppose we can try. What am I going to tell my husband? Yes, of course, that's the least we can do. Thank you for taking me seriously. My husband said I shouldn't call, but there you have it. I did!'

'Well, I can't pretend to understand it all. But it's good just the same. And it's great we've found all those missing animals.'

Chapter 11

The Cat Whisperer Starts to Become a Little Famous

Mr Brown felt a little miffed that his wife had called the police against his advice. But he couldn't stay miffed for very long once it was apparent that Ruby could indeed speak with her cat and a good thing had come from it. Stolen animals had been found and repatriated to their owners.

So he agreed that the policeman could bring out his cat.

Several days later, early on a Saturday morning, DS Adams came to the farm with his little black kitten. Ruby, Mrs Brown, and Penny, greeted him on the front verandah.

'We caught the animal thief, thanks to your daughter,' said the police sergeant, as he got out of his car.

'Oh that's wonderful news,' smiled Mrs Brown. (It was especially wonderful since now she absolutely knew that she was not "loopy".)

'Thanks to your daughter.'

'And my cat!' Ruby reminded him.

DS Adams nodded, 'And your cat', he agreed.

In his arms he cradled the thin, little black kitten. 'Well, this is really kind of you, Ruby.' he said. 'Betty Black has been off her food for weeks but our Vet can't find anything wrong with her.'

'Penny can tell us,' replied Ruby, at which point, Penny, lying in Ruby's arms, flicked her tail and made some 'Brrrh Brrrh' noises.

Betty Black replied with her own chorus of 'Brrrhs'.

Penny responded with more 'Brrrhs', flicking her tail and twitching her ears.

Then Ruby, the *non*-feline, made some "Brrrh' noises of her own and wriggled her eyebrows at Penny.

Finally, Ruby asked the policeman, 'Did someone recently die in your house?'

DS Adams scratched his head. 'No. Nobody died.'

'Well then, perhaps someone went away?'

'Oh? Yes, my mother-in-law finally went home. She had stayed with us for a few months to help my wife with the twins.'

'There it is,' said Ruby. 'Cats can't tell the difference between someone dying and someone leaving. It's all the same to them. Betty Black is *pining* for your mother-in-law.'

'*Pining?*' he asked. 'How does such a young girl, like you, know the meaning of that word? If you don't mind me asking.'

'I read it in my poetry book. It means you are missing someone so badly you are beside yourself with worry and then you can't eat.'

The policeman shook his head slowly. 'What do I do? My mother-in-law lives hundreds of miles away.'

'Did she like to talk to Betty Black?'

'Well yes. Talked to her all the time.'

'There you are. Ask your mother-in-law to phone regularly and chat to Betty Black. Make sure she says all the same words and makes the same sounds as she did when she was staying with you. But also make sure you get her to post you a piece of her clothing, so that her scent is on it. Give that to your cat to sleep on. Then Betty Black will think she's still there and stop pining.'

'Well I'll be …' repeated DS Adams. 'Did your cat tell you that?'

'Yes Sir.'

'Well I'll be!' (he seemed to have a vocabulary deficit, Ruby thought to herself). 'I can't wait to get home and tell my wife. She'll be so relieved! *I'm* so relieved! Can I give you something, Ma'am. Payment?'

'Oh goodness no!' said Mrs Brown. 'We're just happy to help.'

'I know! My wife bakes the best apple pie in town. Do you like apple pie, Ruby?'

'That would be lovely. But you had better bring something for Penny too.'

'What does she like?'

'Chicken necks.'

'Chicken necks and apple pie it will be.' He hurried off stroking Betty Black enthusiastically.

Article from the local Newspaper, *The Wingaroo Post:*

"Animal Circle Farm" Now Cat Whisperer ... what next?

More unusual happenings from the Brown farm. It appears that the identity of a local animal hustler has been made known to police and an arrest has been made. The police have now reunited with their happy owners: 4 dogs, 1 parrot, 3 prize sheep, and a budgerigar. Miss Islington, from Carter's Lane, was so happy to be reunited with her long missing King Charles Cavalier spaniel, that she insisted on taking the Brown family out to dinner. When asked how she knew who the animal thief was, Miss Ruby Brown, the young girl of the family, said it was her cat who told her. This is the first time a cat whisperer has appeared in our Shire, and the first time, as far as we know, that it has occurred in a child.

Of course, this article stirred up a lot of interest. Many people wrote in to *The Wingaroo Post*, advancing their own theories about cat whisperers.

One man was sure that Ruby must have made it all up. She must have seen the thief's van outside the farm gate.

Another man claimed that aliens from outer space had secretly visited Ruby, without her knowing, and bestowed upon her the gift of animal communication.

Then an anonymous writer: the note came in big letters, not typed up on a computer, but handwritten with a pencil. It simply said: *'Here is a message from someone who wants to be called "O". This is what "O" said: "Every human has the ability to communicate with animals. After all, animals from any species can talk with one another, and when you think about it, people belong to the animal kingdom too. People have simply forgotten how to do it, that is all. There is no trickery in it. "O"'*

At school, it was a different matter altogether. Most of the time Ruby had gone unnoticed. No one played with her. No one talked to her, except when Bella had something disparaging to say. At lunch time Ruby always sat by herself, reading her book. But then she started reciting poetry off by heart, which of course was definitely weird. And now that she was in the paper, you might say Ruby was sort of a *person of note*. Things started to change. "Weird" turned into "awesome".

Children, some of whom Ruby had never spoken to, began approaching her saying things like: 'It's so cool being able to talk to animals - I wish I could talk to my blue-tongued lizard'! Or ' Woooh, that's sooooo amazing Ruby, totally cool!'

But the odd thing was that Bella said *nothing* to Ruby. In fact, since their last troubled conversation, Bella had avoided talking to Ruby at all.

The children began asking Ruby to help solve their own animal problems. One girl from Year 9 asked one day, 'My budgerigar keeps saying "Where's the pirate? Where's the pirate?" all day long. He's driving us nuts! Can you find out what he means?'

'You would have to bring him out to our farm and let my cat talk to him,' said Ruby.

A boy from Year 7 asked her if she knew why his dog spent all day chasing his tail and wasn't satisfied until he had finally caught it. But then he'd bite his tail and then scamper away whimpering and hide under the house.

Ruby's reply was the same: 'You'll have to bring him out to our farm and let my cat talk to him.'

Before you knew it, children from Ruby's school were coming to visit Oat Hollow on Saturdays for "Animal Consultations".

Her parents did not mind. As far as they were concerned, other children were taking an interest in Ruby and surely something good would come of it? Maybe Ruby would start having a special friend or two?

The mystery of the morning animal circle continued and Mr Brown quietly found all the attention about his farm and his daughter quite pleasing. He was the father and farmer after all, so he felt he must have had some small part to play in it all. One thing though, only Saturday's for children to come with their animals. Not Sunday, that was family day.

As days went by, adults also started to phone and ask if they could bring their animals for a consultation too. Mr Brown agreed but only on Saturdays.

Chapter 12

The Oracle Teaches the Animals to See the Field of Hum

The Oracle hobbled up slowly at the conclusion of the morning animal circle, burping and passing wind as he went. Then he sat on the ground before everyone, holding his stomach.

'That feels better.'

'Are you alright, Oracle?' asked Penny.

'Yes my dear, just a little ... how shall I say ... flatulent. I suffer from a condition called *Borborygmus*.'

'*Borborygmus?* It sounds like a character out of Shakespeare,' quipped Penny, 'I do hope it is not serious ... or contagious?'

'There are three ailments which inflict suffering on us mortals. One of them is troubles of the digestion. That is my affliction. The other two ...' the animals all inched forward to hear the Oracle's wise words ... 'I can't remember.'

The animals slumped back again.

'Perhaps if you didn't eat so much celery?' suggested Penny meekly.

'Of course. Celery is my nemesis.'

'*Nemesis?*'

'Yes: celery is the inescapable agent of my own downfall.'

'Well, why don't you just stop eating it then?'

'You are right. I could. Yet I don't. Now I suffer. It makes no sense, I agree. *The persistence of habit becomes the tyranny of one's existence.*'

'Is that from one of Ruby's poems?'

'No, that was me, reflecting on my unwise habit. But if I *was* a poet, I'd be quite pleased with that line. Has a good ring to it, don't you think?'

Penny decided it was best to leave the subject of celery alone for now.

The Oracle began: 'You have all been practising your Field of Hum exercises, I can see that. There is one more lesson for you all and that is why I am here. Once this lesson is completed, and Penny is good enough at it, then we hope and pray that Ruby can save our farm.'

The animal congregation murmured optimistically.

'Today I will teach you another way into the Field of Hum ...'.

The animals all placed their paws on each other.

'It does not require physical contact.'

The animals were all in place, their paws against paws, sitting in their circle, so now they removed their paws.

'Does that mean I don't have to be here?' asked Rufus.

'Yes, you have to be here. In fact, you are our perfect subject. And all you have to do is sit still.'

Rufus look very satisfied with himself. 'Me? You *need* me? Well, I guess I can spare some time.'

Ignoring Rufus, the Oracle said, 'You don't always have physical contact with someone, so you have to learn other ways to Mind Meld. Rufus is our subject. And Rufus, you must sit very still.'

'I think I can manage that, your Grace. Provided I don't miss out on breakfast.'

'We shall be finished before breakfast, have no fear. And don't call me "Your Grace"'.

'Yes, Your Worship.'

The Oracle frowned. 'Sit in front of the oak tree. Keep still! You must not move!'

'Can I scratch my fleas first? Then I'll be able to sit quietly.'

'You may.'

'Thank you, Your Honour.'

'I am *not* a member of the judiciary. Don't call me "Your Honour"!' snapped the Oracle.

'What does *Judiciary* mean?' Simone whispered to Miss Davenport.

Miss Davenport shrugged and rolled her eyes.

Rufus had a profoundly enjoyable scratching session, then sat on his hind legs, perfectly still, the massive oak trunk behind him.

'Now my friends, I want you to look at Rufus' head.'

'Yes,' everyone said in unison.

'Henrietta! Stop chewing your cud!' growled the Oracle.

'I'm the perfect subject for this, aren't I?' said Rufus. 'Are you going to draw me? I think my left side is my best profile.' Rufus inclined his face to one side.

'I said you must not move!' growled the Oracle again.

'Sorry your Majesty.'

Ignoring the regal reference, the Oracle said, 'Now pick a spot slightly above Rufus' head, just an inch or two, on the tree trunk behind him, and fix your eyes on that spot.'

'Yes,' murmured everyone.

'Do not move your eyes at all. If you move your eyes you have to start over again. But, keeping your eyes still, relax your vision so you can see his head out of the corner of your field of vision. Don't move your eyes. Don't rush it! It happens all by itself. You don't actually have to *do anything*. The Field of Hum is already there. Just relax but keep your eyes still. Let your field of vision be as wide as you can. You can see Rufus, and the tree, in your peripheral vision, but all the while your eyes are still on the same spot. Tell me when you start to see the Field of Hum.'

No one said anything at all for a good few minutes. Penny was the first. She kept her eyes still, and relaxed, then started to notice a transparent, golden hue, it was a bit like the shape of a candle flame, appearing around Rufus' head. The more she watched and kept her eyes still and relaxed, the stronger the colour became.... It was not a solid colour. It... sparkled!'

'I can see it!' gasped Penny.

'You're looking at the Field of Hum. Describe it to me!'

'Well, it's all sparkly. I can see through it, but it has a vibration. It sort of *hums*.'

'That is correct. The Field of Hum, which humans call the *aura*, looks *the same as it feels*.'

'Is the Field of Hum always yellow?' asked Penny.

'No, it contains all colours within it. As you see the Field of Hum in other animals, you will see that one colour dominates in each animal, depending on the nature of that animal. For instance, animals who are angry carry a red colour. Many humans carry that colour too.'

'Are humans angry?'

'Many humans are angry, yet they do not know why they are angry.'

'Well,' said Rufus, careful not to move anything except his mouth. 'I can't see the point in being angry if you don't know why you're angry!'

'If you listen to your own thoughts all day long, as humans do,' replied the Oracle, 'you forget all about the Hum. Then you get caught up in thoughts like, "What they did to me" and "What I'm going to do to them" and "They should have done this or that" or "They should *not* have done this or that" - well - how can you *not* get angry if that's what's in your head all day?'

'But everyone needs thoughts, don't they? Otherwise you would not think to go and eat your breakfast!' continued Rufus.

'There is no harm in thinking. The harm comes when you believe that all your thoughts are real. A thought has no inherent reality. Just because a thought enters your head that the sun will turn purple, does not make it so.'

'Oh, I can see it now too!' called out Marty, twitching his little grey mouse tail in excitement.

'Me too, me too!,' cried Miss Davenport.

'Yes, I can see it too. It's marvellous!' said Simone.

It's marvellous,
it's marvellous
and we can see it too, it too,
and we can see it too

sang the sheep quartet.

Chirp! Chirp!

A bird had landed on Henrietta's head and sounded the conclusion of the chorus.

'But I don't understand how I can help Ruby save the farm. It seems an awfully daunting task,' sighed Penny.

'When humans remember the Field of Hum, that can change the way they look at things. When you are aware of the Field of Hum, you know that *what you do to others around you, you also do equally to yourself.*'

'I can't say I understand it,' said Penny.

'Can I move now?' asked Rufus. 'I can feel a flea!'

The Oracle nodded.

Rufus scratched again then plodded off to the garbage in search of food, muttering, 'I don't see why we just can't chew holes in their tyres. What's the good of sitting around being quiet and looking at nothing ... makes no sense at all ... it's never going to work ....'

Chapter 13

Spring Arrives and the Magic Begins

The cold grey skies turned a sparkling azure, as Mrs Brown gazed out the window into the flower garden, where Ruby sat, one cat either side of her. Ruby was reading her poetry book to her cats.

Again the violet of our early days
Drinks beauteous azure from the golden sun,
And kindles into fragrance at his blaze;
The streams, rejoiced that winter's work is done,

'It sounds pretty but I don't understand it.' said Simone in a wistful tone.

'You don't have to understand it,' replied Penny, 'All you do is let the *feeling* of it wash over you. Mr Elliott is rejoicing at the coming of Spring, and at the budding of the flowers and arrival of the warmth. You just breathe in the sounds of the words: imagine smelling the fragrances, seeing the colours, hearing birds singing and the bees buzzing. Actually you don't even have to imagine. Just look at all our flowers. Spring is here now and colours are everywhere!'

Ruby looked at Penny. Penny looked at Ruby.

'How can we stop the mining people ruining our garden?' asked Ruby.

Penny placed her paw on Ruby's hand.

'What are you trying to tell me?' asked Ruby.

Penny removed her paw and placed it onto the page of the open book. Ruby copied her, placing the palm of her hand on the other page. Simone watched intently.

The paper was warm to touch under her hand. The sun's warmth too cradled her face. As she looked into Penny's eyes, Penny took her paw off the book, and placed it on top of Ruby's hand. Now Ruby felt the warmth above and beneath her hand. She felt her hand dissolve in a soft, warm glow and she started to feel sleepy.

'We *can* stop them, can't we?' asked Ruby. A single tear landed on the page by Ruby's hand, highlighting the words, *winter's work is done.*

Ruby then felt the softest touch on her hand and glanced down to see a butterfly had landed there.

Simone watched them intently, wondering what was happening.

There was another keeping a watchful eye. Ruby's mother gazed out the kitchen window at Ruby in the garden with her beloved cats. Sometimes she wondered if Ruby spent too much time by herself (well, not really by herself). Maybe she should do more to arrange play days with other children? Maybe she should take Ruby out of the farm and into town more often? These thoughts often ran through her head. But when she gazed out at Ruby this Spring morning, accompanied by her loyal cats, she knew Ruby had all that she needed right here on the farm. But what if their farm was to be taken away. What would happen to Ruby? What would happen to all of them?

Ruby suddenly closed her book and took her basket over her arm. 'Come on Penny, Simone. It's flower picking time!'

It was the first day of her Spring school holidays. Ruby loved these holidays the best. She could watch flowers gently open to the new, warm, fragrant light. And she could spend lots of time with her cats out in the flower garden.

Already her marigolds were just begging to be picked. Ruby just adored orange and gold. Reverently, she placed them in her basket, ready for drying. Penny sniffed and nodded approvingly by twitching an ear and shaking her head: she loved Ruby and she loved these special moments together.

Simone decided to chase butterflies around the garden: it gave her welcome relief from worrying about things.

Flower drying was one of Ruby's favourite things. She rather liked time by herself for such pleasures. She now had four books of pressed flowers and a whole bag full of ones she had dried. These freshly picked ones she placed beside her pillow: this ensured that in her dreams she could breathe in the magic of the marigolds.

That night, she lay on her bed, reading poems to the cats, the freshly picked flowers arranged by her pillow. She had, as she said she would, patiently worked her way through two thirds of the big, old, blue poetry book.

Turning a page, she found another of the mysterious notes, written in the old-fashioned, swirly handwriting.

As you read, always keep your open hand placed against the page.
Let your hand and the book join into one.

Placing her hand on one of the open pages, Ruby imagined her hand sinking down into the book, as though it was a basket full of soft flowers. Then she read this out to the cats, and they blinked at her quietly:

The Time hath laid his mantle by
Of wind and rain and icy chill,
And dons a rich embroidery
Of sunlight poured on lake and hill.

On this Spring night as Ruby lay asleep, dreaming of flowers, Penny breathed in the delicious scents of the freshly picked marigolds, and as usual, gently placed her paw upon Ruby's hand.

The following morning, after breakfast, Mrs Brown went upstairs to find Ruby on her floor with her pencils.

'What are you drawing, Ruby?' she asked.

'I'm drawing the two men who want to dig up our farm.'

'Oh,' her mother replied. Why was Ruby drawing those two men? 'That's nice darling,' was all she could think to say.

What Mrs Brown did not see was what Ruby did when she had finished drawing the men. But Penny and Simone did. They watched as she took two of her dried marigolds and gently cut out the faces of the men she had drawn, and place one face onto each flower.

Then she fixed her gaze on the floor. There was a little spot of fluff on the carpet just beside the pictures. That's where she fixed her eyes, yet without moving her eyes at all, she was able to see the pictures she had drawn in the periphery of her field of vision. The she waited, keeping her eyes still but relaxed.

After a minute a halo of light appeared around the drawings: a golden yellow, with little blue tips at the edges. Still keeping her eyes on the fluff spot, this halo became stronger.

Penny gently placed her paw on Ruby's wrist. Ruby placed her other hand gently on the drawings and imagined her hand passing right through the drawings. After a minute, she had the feeling of her hand going right down through the flowers and into the floor. It was a weird feeling, but she loved it.

Then she said these words:

Here is a gift for you
May you accept it
May you leave our farm in peace
May you see that you don't need any more black stuff
out of the ground
May our beautiful farm remain pristine
May our world be clean and green
May you wake up and see clearly
what you already know deep down
May we all be well and happy.

When Ruby next saw the men who wanted to dig up the farm she went over to say hello. As usual, she was shadowed by Penny and Simone. They were observed first by the sheep, who thought Ruby was coming out to give them hay. Henrietta bleated excitedly and ran after Ruby and the cats. All this happened under the watchful eye of two other inhabitants of the farm. The first, Ruby's mother, watched from the kitchen as Ruby went up to the men and gave them each a dried marigold.

The other watchful eye, beneath which was a knowing smile, belonged to one who publicly called himself "O".

The two men accepted their flowers from Ruby with a mixture of surprise and amusement.

'Thank you,' said one of the men. 'Are these for our wives?'

'Oh no,' replied Ruby calmly, 'I made them especially for you. Carry them with you. Sleep with them beside your pillow.'

'Will the flowers bring us good luck?' quizzed the other man with a distracted smile.

"Oh yes,' replied Ruby truthfully. 'The best luck you have ever had in your whole life, I'm sure of it.'

'Thank you, that's very sweet, we'll do just what you say.'

They chuckled quietly as Ruby went back to the house, but not quietly enough that Penny could not over-hear one of them saying, 'Imagine having the spare time to make something like dried flowers. Sometimes I wish I was a kid again!'

'My kids wouldn't be interested in flowers,' replied the other man. 'I can't get them off their computer screens for a second!'

Watching from the kitchen window, Mrs Brown wondered why she was giving *those* men flowers. She asked Ruby why when she came inside.

'Oh Mummy. We have to save the farm from being dug up and ruined. And those flowers will save the farm.'

Mrs Brown was lost for words. What could she say? 'How will those flowers do that?' she asked.

'It's the magic of the marigolds, Mummy, you'll see. Penny told me what to do ....'

When the mining men came next time, Ruby and the cats were there to greet them again.

'Hey, Sweetie,' said one of the men. 'We forgot to ask your name last time!'

'Ruby.'

'Ruby,' smiled the other man. 'There must be something *special* about those flowers. We were just talking about it. I've had the best sleep in years. My wife said I woke up with a smile on my face.'

'Me too,' said the other man, taking his flower out of his shirt pocket. 'What kind of flowers are they?'

'Marigolds,' said Ruby. 'We have a whole garden of them: you can come and see if you like.'

The two men looked at each other and shrugged. 'Well, why not? As long as your parents don't mind?'

'No! Of course they won't.'

Ruby lead them to her flower garden, shadowed by the cats. 'You can smell all these flowers: marigolds, lavender, nasturtiums, geraniums, love-in-the-mist, over here. And over there,' said Ruby gesturing, 'are our native flowers: guinea flower, boobialla, grevillea, mint bush. We grow them to sell. But the marigolds are especially mine.'

The men followed her around her garden, sniffing, touching, taking in the colours and fragrances, ablaze before them.

'Here, I will pick some marigolds for your bosses,' offered Ruby.

'If my boss could sleep as well as I now do, he'll give me a pay rise,' chuckled one of the men.

'What do your bosses look like, and what are their names?' asked Ruby.

'There are two. Our immediate boss is Frank, he's a bald guy with a moustache and a dimpled chin. Then there's the big boss. He's in charge of the whole company. His name is Mr Southward. He's got round glasses, and his face is all red like a tomato.'

Ruby held the freshly-picked flowers in her hand. Penny entwined herself around Ruby's ankle, then settled at her feet looking up at her.

'First let me tell you a little poem', said Ruby.

'Oh?' The two men looked at each other and again shuffled uncomfortably. 'We have to keep going, really, and what would your mother say, anyway?'

'She won't mind. It will only take a moment. You'll like it.'

'Well I'm sure there's no harm in that!'

'Sit!' beckoned Ruby.

Three people and two cats sat together in a circle, enveloped by a cascade of colours and delicious fragrances. The cats sat either side of Ruby, who held out the flowers to the men, her eyes widened, and for a moment the men thought she was looking right through them.

'Here, put your hands lightly on the flowers and I'll tell you the poem. But if you're going to give something nice to your bosses, it works best if you picture them clearly in your mind.'

The two men looked at each other, a little bemused, shrugged, and said 'Okay!'

Penny had her eyes glued on Ruby, as she spoke the words:

So hush! I will give you this flower to keep;
See, I shut it inside your sweet, cold hand.
There, this is our secret! go to sleep;
You will wake, and remember, and understand.

Then men looked at each other uncomfortably and went to stand up.

'Wait!' said Ruby. 'This next bit I wrote myself.'

They remained seated, as Ruby said these words:

Here is a gift for you
May you accept it
May our world be clean and green
May you wake up and see clearly
What you already know deep down
May we all be well and happy.

The two men awkwardly thanked Ruby and went about their work.

That night at dinner Mrs Brown casually asked why Ruby had given those men *two* lots of flowers.

'Penny told me what to do. We have to get the mining men to change their minds about digging up Oat Hollow. The flowers will help them change their minds.'

Mr Brown glanced up briefly from his paper and grumbled distractedly. He didn't want to think about those troublesome mining people. And he certainly didn't like the idea of Ruby giving *those people* flowers.

'How does Penny know how to do that?' asked her mother.

'Oh, she's been taking lessons from my guinea pig.'

Mr Brown again looked at his wife over the local newspaper, raised an eyebrow, sighed, then resumed reading. Mrs Brown didn't know why, but she quietly felt that something good would come out of this strangeness.

Chapter 14

A Letter Arrives and Oat Hollow is the Subject of Much Attention From the Outside World

'Ruby's done it!' cried Simone excitedly. 'And Penny has done it too, of course!'

Simone was so excited she sprinted around the barn yard to tell everyone, a flash of blurry grey, then sat beside Penny at the oak tree.

The usual assortment of creatures came at once.

'Done what?' grumbled Rufus, very annoyed. 'This had better be good. I was working on my favourite piece of pork rind.'

'We don't need a snapshot into your culinary adventures, thank you,' snapped Miss Davenport.

'I just heard Mr Brown read the letter to Mrs Brown ...' gasped Simone.

Squeals and yelps of delight could be heard from the Brown household. Even Darren, the Brown's farmhand, quickly ran into the house to see what all the fuss was about.

'What's all that commotion about?' asked Miss Davenport.

'The mining people have decided they won't dig up our farm! I heard Mr Brown read out the letter myself. It said something like *Mining exploration on your property has been cancelled*.' Simone felt her eyes water. 'Hoorah our farm is saved!' she gasped.

Our farm is saved,
hoorah hoorah,
our farm is saved today! today!
our farm is saved today!

rang out the sheep chorus, much louder than usual.

It was indeed a day for rejoicing at Oat Hollow. And the word soon spread about town too. The following day a man came out from the local newspaper to interview the Brown family.

Extract from the Wingaroo Times:

Farm Saved from Mining

The Brown Farm is again the subject of mysterious events. First we reported the mysterious circle of animals. Then Ruby Brown suddenly became a cat whisperer. Now …as with many farms in our Shire, mining exploration licences have been issued and many properties are being drilled. But the Brown farm, for some inexplicable reason, has been removed from the list for exploration. Of course the Browns are delighted with this outcome.

We interviewed the Brown family about how they went about getting their farm off the list, because other farmers would like the same too.

'It was my daughter,' said Mrs Brown. 'We don't know how she did it, but she was able to influence the mining people to change their minds.'

When asked how a young girl could bring about such a great change, Mrs Brown said it was a "mystery" to her too.

But privately, she knew that Penny had told Ruby what to do.

The school yard was all abuzz. Now Ruby had saved her farm, the teenagers looked upon her, not as weird, or even slightly awesome, but as *majorly* awesome.

Then a *most* surprising thing happened: Bella suddenly came to talk to Ruby at lunch time.

'Hi Ruby, mind if I sit next to you?' Bella asked.

'No, I don't mind,' Ruby was surprised. Then she added, 'I won't try to read you a poem though, I think that might have upset you last time.'

Bella bit her lip, then exhaled a long sigh. 'Ruby. I was like, a real cow to you. I know I was.'

Ruby was about to explain that a cow is a friendly, benign animal that provides sustenance to millions, so the analogy was not really apt, but Bella held her hand up.

'No, let me finish. You *were* right. Things are really bad at my place. Mum and Dad are yelling at each other. Then next they're not talking at all. It's the pits. I think they're going to split up.'

'Gee, sorry to hear that, Bella'.

'There's something you can do to help. But I won't blame you if you say No. I don't deserve anything from you after I treated you so bad.'

'How can I help?'

'*Can you save our farm too*? It's about to get mined. Mum and Dad have gone ballistic! I'm sure if we can stop our farm getting mined, that will fix their stress. And then things will go back to normal again.'

'Yes, I guess so.'

Bella studied Ruby closely.

'Just like that? You said "Yes" just like that? After how I treated you? I can't figure you out! Why would you help me after I was so mean?'

'Were you? I just thought you were upset. And now I can see why.'

'I just can't believe you're real. I don't know anybody else like you.'

'I'm definitely real. And now we're friends, don't you think?'

'Yeah, I guess we are!'

'Why don't you come over to my house on Saturday? Draw a picture of the mining men that you have seen. Find out their names. I know the names of their bosses already. And bring that stuff with you. And when we've sorted out your farm, *you* can help *me* with a bigger job.'

'What's that?'

'Oh,' said Ruby matter-of-factly, ' we have to save the *whole* Shire.'

Bella's jaw dropped again. Ruby started to wonder if Bella had an issue with her temporo-mandibular joint.

'*Who told you that you have to save the whole Shire?*'

'My cat, Penny.'

'What does the Shire need saving *from*?'

'Same thing as *our* farms. It's all getting dug up. And the trees could get chopped down. And dirty air.'

'But how can *we* stop all that?'

'Come over to mine and I'll show you.'

Bella contemplated for a moment - 'Was it your cat Penny that taught you how to save *your* farm?'

Ruby nodded.

Bella nodded. 'Count me in. I'll be there.'

The week after the article in the local paper, a man from the TV station came to interview Ruby. Mr Brown had given permission for the interview, provided that the TV reporter only asked questions that other children could understand (no adult words), and on condition that the farm location was kept secret. He didn't want "everyone under the sun" coming to the farm and unsettling the animals.

Ruby said she wanted to be interviewed too. This was quite surprising because people thought she was a quiet, shy, little girl, who didn't like lots of fuss. But she said it was "really important".

The TV man wore a dark suit, polished shoes and a red tie. Ruby noticed that his right shoe lace had come undone.

'Can I see your microphone?' asked Ruby.

He handed over his microphone.

Examining the microphone, Ruby asked, 'Can you use your own fist as a microphone?'

'No, that wouldn't work. Now can I ask you some questions, Ruby?'

Nodding, she handed the microphone back.

He talked into the camera: 'I'm at the Brown Farm, which is in the Wingaroo Shire, and I'm talking to Miss Ruby

Brown. She is somewhat of a celebrity in this town because she can talk to animals. But that's not all. She has somehow managed to save her family's farm from being mined. And we are going to find out how she did it.'

He turned to Ruby.

'We understand that you can communicate with your cat?' he asked, talking into his microphone (not his fist). 'What exactly have you learnt from your cat?'

'About the Field of Hum.'

The reporter glanced around the farm. 'The Field of … *which field is that?*'

'It's everywhere.'

'What do you *do* with it?'

'You don't *do* anything with it. You just notice it. Once you start noticing it, things start to change.'

'But if it's everywhere, why can't we see it?'

'You can see it. You just have to learn how to *look*.'

The man shifted uncomfortably and smiled into the camera.

'What's the most important thing your cat has told you?'

'All about saving the Shire,' said Ruby.

'You mean, saving your *farm*?' he corrected.

'No,' said Ruby, 'that was easy. Now we have to save the *whole Shire*.'

The TV man made an *adult* smile, 'That sounds like a very big job for one young girl.'

'My friend Bella is going to help me.'

'How will you go about saving the Shire?'

'I am making special, dried flowers. When they are ready I will send them to all the farms in the district. The Oracle said this would save the Shire.'

'And who is the Oracle?'

'My guinea pig.'

The man hesitated, a little stumped what to ask next.

'Why does your cat think the Shire needs saving?'

'She says all the farms are going to get dug up. This will ruin everything. People and animals might have to leave their homes. She said people fight and argue about the black stuff and the funny thing is we don't need it at all. We just think we do.'

'And what should the farmers do with the flowers you send?'

'That's the easy part. They give them to the mining people. The mining people just have to wear them, or put them in their pockets during the day or beside their pillows at night. If they do that, the Oracle says it will save the Shire.'

'But how will that work?'

'Your right shoe lace is undone. Better do it up before you trip,' replied Ruby.

Losing his focus for a minute, he gazed down at his shoe. When he looked up, Ruby had disappeared into the flower garden.

'Well,' the TV man cleared his throat and grinned into the camera. 'Today I am at the Brown farm. I am not permitted to say where the farm is. This young girl called Ruby Brown has told us how she is going to save the whole of the Shire. So to all of you farmers out there, when your special flowers arrive, you'd better make sure you follow your instructions!' he said in a *serious* tone but with a knowing twinkle in his eye.

Chapter 15

The Sheep Swoon and Simone Has Her Own Private Audience With the Oracle

'Can you tell us one of the poems out of Ruby's book?' Miss Davenport asked Penny, as everyone was arriving for their morning circle.

'Yes, what a perfect idea. But first I have to ask you something.'

'Yes, my dear?'

'Well, we've been practising Mind Meld, by touching each others paws, and entering the Field of Hum that way. It's going well I think. Except for one little thing.'

'What's that, dear.'

'Everyone has had a go with everyone else, except you and Rufus.'

'But he smells. He's dirty. And he has no manners.'

'There's a greater concern here, Miss D. And that's saving the Shire. If we can't all be in harmony, how will we work together to save the Shire?'

Miss Davenport turned to lick the side of her ample rump in irritation.

'Very well,' she muttered. 'We must all put in a proper effort. I will do it for the greater good!'

When Miss Davenport approached Rufus, his little, ginger ears peeled back ready for the usual stern rebuke.

'This morning,' the boss sheep said awkwardly, ' you are to place your paw on *my* hoof.'

Rufus regarded her cautiously. Was this a ploy to find another reason to growl at him? Carefully, he placed his tiny paw on her front hoof and they sat down beside each other. Miss Davenport glanced at him briefly, with a mixture of irritation and *awkwardness*.

Penny spoke up. 'Miss Davenport has requested that we start with a poem before we do our Mind Meld. Now let's see what I can remember. Oh I know! Listen to this one by Mr Keats:

> *I met a lady in the meads,*
> *Full beautiful – a fairy's child,*
> *Her hair was long, her foot was light,*
> *And her eyes were wild*

As Penny recited these words, the other sheep, standing behind the little circle, closed their eyes, chewing their cuds contentedly, and swayed and swooned to the soothing words. But they swayed and swooned so much, that they toppled over like a line of dominos.

'That is lovely, dear,' praised Miss Davenport, looking over her shoulder as the other sheep picked themselves up again. 'Perhaps something less *swoony* might be better.'

'Oh I know another one that is definitely *not swoony*. It's by Mr Blake.'

Fur billowing in the gentle breeze, Penny stood on her hind legs, one paw held against the oak tree. Brandishing the other paw before her, she gestured grandly, but then noticed she had again missed a spot on that paw, so hurriedly licked it clean.

I was angry with my friend;
I told my wrath, my wrath did end.
I was angry with my foe:
I told it not, my wrath did grow.

And I watered it in fears,
Night and morning with my tears:
And I sunned it with smiles,
And with soft deceitful wiles.

And it grew both day and night.
Till it bore an apple bright.
And my foe beheld it shine,
and he knew that it was mine.

And into my garden stole,
When the night had veil'd the pole;
In the morning glad I see;z
My foe outstretched beneath the tree.

After digesting this long poem, Rufus was the first to speak.

'Why is his enemy lying under the apple tree like that? Why doesn't he just climb up and eat the apples? I'm sure I would.'

'Oh yes, why not eat the apples?' Henrietta agreed. 'What a waste just to leave them there like that.'

'I know exactly what Mr Blake means,' said Simone in a serious tone. 'He got all angry and upset and frightened, but instead of telling someone so he could make it better, he kept it all locked up inside his head. And the longer he kept it locked up inside the bigger it grew, until in the end it grew into a big, twisted thing like a tree. But its apples were sour and poisonous to anyone who tried them. And his poor enemy ended up eating one and died! I know just what he means! You get something horrible into your head and then you just can't get it out. That happens to me all the time!' bemoaned the sleek, sensitive, Siamese. 'I think he wrote that poem just for me!'

Everyone watched in dismay as Simone grew more distressed.

'It's alright,' volunteered Marty mouse, 'it's only a poem.'

'Simone,' said Penny, 'I didn't mean to upset you. I suppose Mr Blake can be rather visual, a little sinister. He's a bit too strong for some.'

'I've had another *seeing*, worse than before', sobbed Simone. '*And it scares me.*'

'You are having too many seeings, my dear,' decided Miss Davenport. 'This won't do. You can't go on like this.'

'I think Simone should go and see the Oracle,' Marty volunteered. 'He'll know what to do.'

'Tell us all about your seeing', offered Penny gently. 'I'm sure you'll feel better if you do.'

'It's all full of blackness, and cold winds, and being all

alone in the dark, with no one to run to for comfort, and no where to go.'

'That sounds like this end of the world nonsense,' said Rufus. 'I heard the Oracle talking to Penny about it. Could you tell if there's anything nice to eat at the end of the world?'

'Or luscious grass?' asked Henrietta.

'I hope the end of the world is not a dirty place', muttered Miss Davenport to herself.

'Oh stop it everyone! You don't understand how awful this is! The end of the world means there is *nothing left*! We won't be together any more! Can you imagine how horrible that would be?'

'Let's take her to the Oracle at once,' repeated Marty in a desperate tone. 'He'll know what to do.

Penny and Rufus postponed their morning parade of "proud cat with freshly caught rat", since Simone's distress was more urgent. And that was a bit of a shame, because Mr Brown had invited the Taylors over to breakfast. He wanted to show off how efficient *his* cat was at cleaning up the rats in the barn. All the Brown family, plus the Taylors, were sitting on the front verandah, finishing their coffee and awaiting the spectacle.

However, on this particular morning, an *unexpected* spectacle greeted them.

Penny and Marty (a marsupial mouse, and *not* a rat, Mr Brown was quick to point out to Mr Taylor), were guiding Simone, their pretty Siamese, by a front paw each, across the yard and into the guinea pig hutch.

'That's the darn, weirdest thing I've ever seen,' said Mr Taylor. 'What the heck are those animals up to?'

Mr Brown sat back in his chair with a superior air of satisfaction. 'That, my friend, is one of the great mysteries of this farm ...'.

'It's not really a mystery, Daddy,' piped up Ruby. 'The guinea pig teaches the cats what to do.'

'How on earth does a guinea pig know so much?' quizzed Mr Taylor.

'Penny says, "He's an old soul". I'm not really sure what that means ...'.

'Who's Penny?'

'My cat,' motioned Ruby, 'over there going into the guinea pig hutch.'

'How on earth can a cat be friends with *a mouse and a guinea pig*? It makes no sense!'

Mr Brown chuckled, pleased with himself. 'Lot's of things on this farm make no sense. Haven't you read the local paper? And you know what? I don't mind. It feels good. You'll see.'

'Well,' said Mr Taylor. 'let's make some sense out of what we can do about these mining companies coming into our Shire. We have the best farming land in the whole country. It'd be criminal to dig it all up!'

Mr Taylor shot a question at Ruby: 'How on earth did you get the mining people to change their mind?'

'Flowers and poems,' answered Ruby truthfully.

'How on earth ...' Mr Brown raised up his hand to stop Mr Taylor saying any more *how on earths*.

'Ruby is planning to save everyone's farms. I don't know how she saved ours. But she did. If she did it once then maybe she can do it again. Best not to ask too many questions.'

'Hmmf,' said Mr Taylor. 'If Ruby saves *my* farm I'll... oh I don't know what I'll do ...'.

While this conversation was taking place among the people, a very different one was taking place within the guinea pig hutch.

'Miss Simone, your Excellency,' announced little Marty, as he ushered the fearful cat into the hutch, retreating backwards out the door, bowing so low that his nose was all but on the ground. But in his solemnity, his bottom bumped into the doorway with a crash.

'I beg your pardon, oh Infinite One.'

The Oracle waved him away with a flourish of his paw. 'I wish he wouldn't call me "Infinite One". It's quite irritating, you know. The only thing *infinite* about me is the size of my belly .'

Marty reverently closed the door and waited outside with Penny.

'I have come for help, Sir.' said Simone, meekly.

'You can call me Ollie.'

'Ollie?' Simone, a little surprised, nearly forgot about being all upset. 'Isn't that a bit… familiar?'

'It's a special name just for you to use.'

'Well …thank you,' Simone curtsied.

'No need for formalities here, my dear. We are very casual. Although I wouldn't say that about a certain marsupial mouse.'

'I have come to you for help,' she whimpered.

'Yes I know.'

'How do you know?'

'You're always scared, aren't you?'

'Yes. Every day I think something *bad* will happen. I wish I was more like Rufus. He never worries about anything. Except food.'

'That my dear is your *problem*. And it is a common problem these days. You let *everything* come inside.'

'What do you mean?'

'Rufus only concerns himself with food. That is *his* preoccupation. That is all he thinks about - correct?'

'Yes.'

'You let everything from the outside world come into your mind and heart. The feelings, worries, thoughts, preoccupations, forebodings of the world. Your door is always open to them.'

'What door?'

'Your mind. Your space. Your field of awareness. You let everything in 24 hours a day. And none of it belongs to you. It belongs to others. You mistake it for your *own*.'

'How do I shut the door on it?'

The Oracle instructed: 'Imagine a big cone of bright light all around you. The brightest light you ever saw, even more powerful than the sun. It is so bright, and so strong, nothing can possibly pass through. You are the only one inside this cone. If something tries to come in, it just bounces right off again. Now when you are in this protective circle of light your door is closed. Close your door when you are scared. Especially close it just before you go to sleep, because that's when the things you don't want can sneak in.'

Feeling a little calmer, Simone said, 'Sometimes things come in which are important. It was I who knew that Penny was in danger. And now, I am seeing pictures about *the end of the world*.'

'Pictures about the future are just an *imagining*. The only real thing is what happens in front of your nose…'.

Simone calmed down as she started to listen to the Oracle.

'What is scary in this moment?' he continued. 'All that's

happening is you are talking to a fat, gluttonous, old guinea pig.'

'You make it sound so easy,' said Simone hesitantly, 'and comforting at the same time.'

'It is easy and simple. Only thinking about it makes it complicated. Just make the protection circle of bright light in your imagination, like I have explained. Nothing else is needed. Don't start thinking about it. The longer you hold the picture of your circle in your imagination, the stronger your door is closed. And stop thinking about the future.'

'Will I have this fear forever?' she asked.

The Oracle looked at her for a long while before answering.

'Tell me where you feel frightened. Where in your body.'

'It's a horrible, tight lump right here in my tummy,' Simone pointed with her paw. 'Like I had swallowed a hard ball and it was stuck there.'

'Now I am going to answer your question,' replied the Oracle. 'You won't understand it yet. But one day I will show you.'

Simone nodded, quivering, half in expectation, half in fear.

'One day you'll be able to look inside that ball that you have in your tummy. And when you can look inside that ball, do you know what you will find there?'

Simone shook her head, holding her paws at her ears in despair, tears in her eyes.

'You will find the most beautiful, peaceful and loving place in the whole, wide world. It's hiding away right there, inside that scary ball in your tummy, just waiting for you to look inside.'

'I wouldn't dare try to look inside it. It's too scary!'

'Yes you can. No it's not. And one day I will show you how.'

'When?'

'As soon as you can get the circle of light working properly. Then I will show you. First, you stop the bad stuff coming in. Next, you look into the place inside you where the fear is and the fear changes into its opposite: *love.*'

'Oh I wish I'd come to speak with you years ago… but I was always a bit scared of you.'

'And now that you have met me, are you still frightened?'

'No, I suppose not. Actually, now you seem familiar to me, like an old friend I haven't seen for ages. Or like a grandfather.'

'And what do you now see before you?'

'Hmmm,' thought Simone carefully, 'a wise being?'

'Goodness me no! What you see before you is an old, overweight guinea pig, with a fat bottom, who eats too much farinaceous food and passes wind too frequently.'

Then something happened which no one had seen before: Simone giggled.

But a sudden clap of thunder wiped the smile off her face as she darted out of the hutch, through the rain and back to the farmhouse.

Chapter 16
Bella Comes to Visit

'I've never seen Ruby so excited,' said Mrs Brown to her husband. 'At least not outwardly.'

Ruby was giggling, jumping and and running to and fro through the house, along the same track in the carpet where her father had anxiously paced only a week before.

'This is the first time she's had a friend come over. And she never laughs about anything. At school, Miss Milner says she's suddenly everyone's friend. The other kids are talking to her. Isn't it wonderful ...?' She burst into tears.

Mr Brown put his arm around his wife and drew her close. He had felt so stressed about the farm, he had forgotten how stressed his wife must have felt too. 'Our little girl has been touched by an angel ...' he whispered in her ear.

Mrs Brown studied him through her watery eyes, 'It's ever since she found that old poetry book.'

'What poetry book?'

'The big, old blue one - *Library of World Poetry*. It was in the attic.'

'I can remember those boxes of books up there when I was a boy. They've probably been in our family for decades. No idea where they came from. So what's so special about the poetry book?'

'Not sure. She found it in the Autumn, and not long after, her teacher, Miss Milner, called to say she could see a big change in Ruby. It must be *something* to do with that book. What else could it be?'

'And since the Autumn,' Mr Brown reminded her, 'our animals have behaved very *strangely*. Ruby started talking *cat* language. Stolen animals have been found thanks to our daughter and one cat. Our farm has been saved. I don't understand it. That book has brought an angel into our house.'

Mrs Brown studied her husband and thought: *something is changing in him too - it's wonderful!*

Ruby skipped to the front gate when she saw Bella being dropped off.

'Bella! Come and see my animals!'

'I wish my Dad would let *me* have animals,' Bella moaned.

'Here', said Ruby leading Bella into the rabbit pen. 'You

hold her like this, your arm crooked, and let her nestle her nose under your arm. Then she feels safe and she won't wriggle. Like this!' Ruby showed her.

Bella's face beamed as she carefully held the rabbit. 'This is awesome! I want one!'

'Now, come and see my guinea pig.'

'Is this the guinea pig who teaches your cat?'

'Yeah!' nodded Ruby with a smile. 'You hold him the same way, then he won't try and get away.'

'I don't get it. Like, how can this animal teach your cat about saving farms? How weird is that!'

'Sure, it's weird,' Ruby shrugged. 'But who cares!'

'I guess *weird* is the new cool!'

Both girls smiled at that idea.

'Let's go and feed the sheep now.'

They took the oats bucket out into the field and sat on a log. With Henrietta leading the mob, the sheep came over to investigate. When she saw the oats bucket, Henrietta bleated and beamed with pleasure, jumping up and down. You'd think she wore springs on her feet.

'Hold your hand *flat*, like this, and keep your thumb out of the way,' instructed Ruby, grabbing a handful of oats and holding her hand out with the offering of oats. 'If you don't keep your thumb flat and out of the way, they'll mistake your thumb for food and you'll soon know about it!'

Bella copied Ruby. 'I want animals just like yours.'

'You can visit mine every Saturday. Mum and Dad won't mind.'

'Really. Can I? You'd let me? I'd love to!'

'That's settled then.'

Bella grinned from ear to ear, then became still and thoughtful. She couldn't believe she was at Ruby's farm. She couldn't believe this strange girl was suddenly her friend.

'Ruby, I don't get it. Like, how can you understand what your cat says? How does it work?'

Ruby frowned as she thought hard about it, then shrugged. 'I don't know. It just happened one day. I just listen to her with a *different* part of my head.'

'Well, it's weird but it worked. You saved your farm. You found those stolen animals. I don't care if it's weird. I don't even care if kids at school think *I'm* weird. I just want to save *my* farm too.'

Ruby sprang into action: 'Let's go to *my* room and get started then.'

Ruby's bedroom was upstairs. At the top of the stairs you turned right and then first left. It was an unusual room. Two ceilings met in the centre then sloped all the way to the floor on either side like a big 'A' frame. One ceiling was blue, the other peach.

They sat on the floor. The two cats, sleeping on Ruby's bed, jumped off and sat close to the girls to watch.

'Do you think we're going to be besties?' asked Ruby.

Bella's face lit up into a supreme smile.

'Yes, I think we could.'

'Great! I've never had a bestie!'

'Me neither.'

'I thought you had lots of friends at school!' said Ruby.

'Well. I kinda do. But no one is a real friend. I don't get invited over to people's places much.'

'Me neither! That makes us the same!'

Bella beamed again.

'How many mining men pictures did you draw?' asked Ruby

'Two'.

Ruby placed them on the floor, then took two of her dried marigolds and placed those on the pictures.

'Is this like, you know, witchcraft, or voodoo, or something?' whispered Bella.

'No. It's just the power of the nature. I'll show you. Look at the flowers, but *don't* look at the flowers.'

'Like wh...a...a...t?"

'Fix your eyes on a spot *near* the flowers, then relax and wait. Don't move your eyes. Soon you will see the flowers even though you're not looking directly at them.'

The two girls sat quietly for a minute or two.

'Oh yeah!' exclaimed Bella in surprise. 'It's like a ... you know ... after image or something like that. Like an orange halo around the flower - right?'

'Yes. We call it the Field of Hum. Keep your eyes still.'

'Who's "we"?'

'Me and my cat.'

Ruby then gently placed each hand lightly on the flower, and also looked at a point near the flowers but not right at them.

'What are you doing?'

'Entering the flowers. You'll see.'

'Man, this creeps me out!'

'No it's not scary. It's really nice. Anyone can do it. You can enter the Field of Hum with your seeing or you can enter with your touch. If you do both, it's better.'

Then Ruby recited her little poem:

Here is a gift for you
May you accept it
May you leave our farm in peace
May you see that you don't need any more black stuff
from the ground.
May our beautiful farm remain pristine.
May our world be clean, green and pristine
May you wake up and see clearly
what you already know deep down
May we all be well and happy.

'That's all done,' Ruby said matter of factly. Then she gently picked up the flowers and put them into a little box for Bella, with some extras for the men's bosses.

'Now when you give these to the mining men, it's best if you recite another little poem. I'll write it down for you. It's out of my poetry book. Penny chose it. Recite it to yourself before you give them the flowers, and if you get the chance, you can recite it for the men too.

Ruby wrote her new poem on some paper for Bella:

So hush! I will give you this flower to keep;
See, I shut it inside your sweet, cold hand.
There, this is our secret! go to sleep;
You will wake, and remember, and understand.

'Is that all we have to do?' quizzed Bella

'That's what *I* did. And you *know* how it turned out.'

'That's awesome. But *creepy*.'

Chapter 17
Sanctuary, Awakening, Renewal

To everyone else it was a day like any other. But in one particular bedroom, on a farm called Oat Hollow, two girls were busy cutting out pictures from a large collection of assorted newspapers and magazines.

Mrs Brown frequently popped her head around the doorway to watch them. When Ruby had announced on television that she was going to save the Shire, Mrs Brown didn't know what to think. No one did. But look at all the strange and wonderful things that had happened already. Why stop now? In fact, she could not resist being embroiled in the single-minded purpose of the girls. She wanted to be a part of it too. She didn't quite know why, she just did. Maybe it reminded her of when she had been a girl, when all the wonders of life lay ahead, waiting to be discovered. But as she grew older, those wonders seemed to have quietly dissolved and life had become routine and predictable. Now, here was something magical .... What did her husband say? Ruby has been "touched by an angel!" Well, something like that had certainly happened but no one could explain it.

When Mrs Brown next looked in, her first inclination was to call her husband to quickly come and see. But no, he had endured enough surprises and disturbances lately, and calling him might just disturb the tranquility and solemnity of the scene.

What she saw was this: magazines and newspapers lay spread open all over the floor. The two girls were cutting out photographs. But this was the most surprising thing of all: the pages of magazines were being quietly turned over by *Penny and Simone*. Gently, one page at a time, one paw at a time, *the cats searched through the magazines until they found what they wanted*. Once something was found, a cat sound something like 'Brrrh ...?' alerted the girls that here was something noteworthy.

At first Mrs Brown thought she was just daydreaming. She rested against the hall wall and took a breath. Surely she did not see what she just saw? She turned to look in the door again and still the cats were turning pages.

Maybe this is a dream. Maybe my whole life is a dream, thought Mrs Brown.

Even though there was a full day's work to do, she asked: 'Can I help too?'

'Oh, would you Mummy? That would be lovely,' replied Ruby. 'We're not sure about all of the faces. We know some faces, like famous prime ministers and presidents. But we don't know everyone. And we're not just looking for world leaders, but other important people. What's the word that Penny used?'

'She said *influential* people', chimed in Bella.

'Yes that's it. *Influential* people. We don't really know what that means, but can you help us choose some *influential* people?'

'Oh yes, I know what Penny means. She means people who run the big corporations, and important people whose opinions are always listened to.'

Before she knew it, Mrs Brown was sitting on the floor, a cat either side of her, searching through magazines with the two girls. Had she not been swept up in the energy and excitement of saving the Shire, she may have paused to think that if her husband could see her now he would say something like, 'Have you all gone *completely* loopy?'

Mr Brown had had a very busy morning. He had drenched all the sheep, which takes longer than you'd imagine because sheep always try to escape, even though they know you won't hurt them and it's for their own good. And sometimes half of the drench ended up on his own clothes because sheep won't always be still. Then he had been mending fences: a never-ending job on a farm.

When he staggered in for lunch he was absolutely exhausted and famished. Taking off his hat, he sat at the kitchen table as usual and read the morning's paper, waiting for his meal to arrive. But since no meal arrived, nor was there any activity in the kitchen, he crept over to the sideboard and picked up the newspaper cutting which had reported on Ruby's animal whispering. He had read it a hundred times already, but loved to read it all again when no one was watching. Not that he was sentimental, mind you.

When he had finished rereading the article and neither meal nor family had appeared, he got up to investigate the cause of this little irritation. Upstairs he found everyone in Ruby's room. At the curious sight before him, he went to push his hat back on his head, having completely forgotten that he always removed his hat when he came inside.

'What on earth …?'

"Oh hello Daddy! We're getting ready to save the Shire.'

"Hello Mr Brown,' said Bella, distractedly.

What met his eyes were rows and rows of dried flowers. Beneath each was a photograph. On the other side of the room was his wife, two cats and Bella, cutting out pictures and browsing magazines.

'Oh!' Mrs Brown said, shocked at herself. 'I completely forgot your… *our* lunch!'

'Dad: come and help us!' cried Ruby.

'Help you? Me? What about lunch?' he said uncertainly.

'Oh please, Dad. It won't take long.'

His wife studied him as he tried to decide what to say. His stomach clearly wanted him in the kitchen but another part of him called him to stay. Still another part of him said *this is silly, childish stuff.* He looked at Ruby. He looked at his wife. They both returned his gaze.

'Well, just for a few minutes then,' he said, and his wife felt a rush of joy.

When Darren came in to collect his wages at the end of the day, the front door of the house was ajar.

'Hello?' he called out. 'Anyone home?'

When no reply came, he thought there must be something wrong. He collected his shovel and held it out, creeping from one room to the next. You never can be too sure, he thought, what with an animal hustler recently caught, maybe he had an accomplice still roaming around trying to steal something?

But there was no one downstairs, not a single sign of life. So he crept quietly up the stairs. One or two steps creaked under his feet, so he went along extra slowly.

He poked his head around Ruby's doorway, one hand on his shovel in case of danger. But when his eyes saw what was happening within, he silently pushed his hat far back on his head (fortunately he had not previously removed it).

'What are you doing with that shovel in the house, Darren?' exclaimed Mr Brown who was sitting on the floor helping cut out photos.

What Darren discovered was the entire Brown family, including the two cats and Bella, arranging flowers and photos in long lines along the floor. There must have been hundreds of them: it was quite a sight! Four lines of flowers stretched across the floor. Mr Brown, Mrs Brown, Ruby and Bella were carefully sliding photos of people one under each flower. On Ruby's desk stood over a hundred packages each addressed to various destinations around the Shire and some for overseas.

Penny and Simone strolled quietly between the lines of flowers, quietly sniffing and examining each flower in turn.

Penny glanced up at Darren as he stared at the scene in disbelief and said, 'Brrrh!'

Darren continued to scratch his head and repeated his mantra: 'I never seen nothing like this'.

'Here Darren,' said Mr Brown. 'Would you collect all those piles of old magazines and put them out by the compost? There's a good bloke. And for goodness sake get rid of that shovel!'

The Brown family, with Bella and Darren, sat out on the verandah as the sun sank low and sprinkles of pink and blue hue settled over the fields. Since Darren was now privy to the peculiar activities at Oat Hollow, he had been invited to stay for dinner. He was rarely invited to dinner, so was very happy about that. But his happiness was not quite as much as that felt by Mrs Brown. She loved to see that her shy, young daughter had involved them all in this wonderful project. Even more, she loved seeing her husband involved in it too.

Ruby sat on her father's knee as they quietly watched the day's colours fade.

Ruby's dad was the first to break the quietude.

'How do you know what you know?' he asked.

Ruby gazed up at her dad.

'My cat told me, of course.'

'So ... what happens next?'

'The flowers now have to be *imbued*,' said Ruby. 'It will take me three days to get everything ready. Then we can all *imbue* the flowers together and post them all off.'

No one really knew what *imbued* meant but they were keen to find out.

'Can Bella come back again for dinner in three days?' asked Ruby.

'Of course my little darling girl,' beamed Mr Brown. 'Of course she can.'

His wife regarded him with quiet, watery eyes.

'Are you alright Mrs Brown?' asked Bella.

Mrs Brown nodded and smiled: 'Just over-happy, that's all.'

What Ruby did in those three nights in her room to prepare to *imbue* her flowers, remained largely a mystery to her family and friends.

That night, while the cats lay sleeping either side of her, Penny's paw as usual on her hand, Ruby was again visited by the strange lady who stood looking out to sea. But this time, she turned her face more towards Ruby. It was a familiar face. A *kind* face.

'Do you not recognise me?' she smiled quietly.

'No. Well I sort of do. And I sort of don't', replied Ruby.

'Here,' said the strange, kind woman. 'Let me place my hand upon yours, then you *shall* remember.'

When she rested her hand on Ruby's it was soft and silky and warm.

'You have learnt your craft well, my child. There will be renewal of all the world…' and with that Ruby woke up. She gazed around her room, not wanting to move, wanting to keep the kind lady close. Then she felt Penny's soft, warm paw on her own hand and drifted back into sleep.

After dinner the following evening Ruby went up to her room, the two cats at her heels. To prepare for imbuing of the flowers, she took three sheets of brand new paper, and on each she drew a big circle in yellow crayon.

On the first sheet of paper, Ruby wrote the word, *Sanctuary* within the circle.

On the second sheet, she wrote, *Awakening*, within the circle.

On the third sheet she wrote, *Renewal,* within the circle.

Earlier in the day, she had found three little amber glass bottles, each with glass droppers screwed in the top. She had filled each one with water from the duck pond. Now she labelled each of the bottles:

First bottle: *Sanctuary*

Second bottle: *Awakening*

Third bottle: *Renewal*

She placed her Sanctuary bottle of pond water within the first circle, just below the word Sanctuary. Then Penny sat beside her and told her what to say:

> Away, away, from men and towns,
> To the wild wood and the downs, –
> To the silent wilderness
> Where the soul need not repress
> Its music, lest it should not find
> An echo in another's mind
> Where the touch of nature's art
> Harmonises from heart to heart.

On the second night, just before bed, Ruby placed the *Awakening* bottle of pond water on the second sheet of paper, within the circle, just beneath the word, *Awakening*. Once again Penny sat by her and told her what to say:

> For now Winter's rains and ruins are over,
> And all the season of snows and wrongs;
> The days dividing lover and lover,
> The light that loses, the night that throngs;
> And time remembered is grief forgotten,
> And frosts are slain and flowers begotten,
> And in green underwood and cover
> Blossom by blossom, the Spring now begins.

On the third night, just before bed, Ruby placed the *Renewal* bottle of pond water into the third circle, just below the word, *Renewal*, and again Penny instructed Ruby what to say:

Come to these scenes of peace,
Where, to rivers murmuring,
The sweet birds all the summer sing,
Where cares and toil and sadness cease!
Stranger, does thy heart deplore
Friends whom thou wilt see no more?
Does thy wounded spirit prove
Pangs of hopeless, severed love?
Thee the stream that gushes clear,
Thee the birds that carol near,
Shall soothe, as silent thou dost lie
And dream of their wild lullaby;
Come to bless these scenes of peace,
Where cares and toil and sadness cease.

After the third night, it was time for the family (and Darren and Bella) to help with the *imbuing* of the flowers.

'Everyone can help, taking it in turns.' said Ruby, picking up the *Sanctuary* bottle. 'All you have to do is think very clearly about our planet being a peaceful place, with no fighting, or arguments, or wars. No ruining of the planet with nasty chemicals, no polluted oceans, no digging holes everywhere, no chopping down all the trees or burning forests. Picture everyone smiling, happy and being friendly to each other. While you hold that picture in your mind, you place a drop of water on each flower, like this...' Ruby dipped the glass dropper into the little water bottle, then filled it up with the imbued water. Then she closed her eyes to make the picture in her head. Then, nodding to herself, she gently dropped a little drop of water, one by one, on to each of the dried flowers, under which still sat a cut out photograph of many presidents and prime ministers (and other *influential* people).

'There are three bottles, each flower gets one drop from each,' she solemnly instructed.

Carefully, everyone had a go, taking a dropper, filling it up, thinking their special thoughts, and placing a drop on each flower.

Then each flower was carefully placed into its addressed package. Every farm in the Shire was getting one. And many were being posted overseas to Presidents and Prime Ministers.

Along with each flower was a letter:

> Dear Friend
> Here is a special flower made just for you.
> It is imbued with peace, and love, and healing.
> Carry it with you by day,
> Place it by your pillow at night.
> It will help you to sleep in peace, and feel happy by day.
> May all beings be happy.
> From your special friend.
> Ruby Brown (and Bella)
> (and the Cats)
> (and the Oracle)

Chapter 18

The End of the World

The Oracle sat before the morning meeting of animals at the oak tree. What was conspicuously absent was any sign of celery or carrot.

Before anyone asked, the Oracle shrugged in resignation and said: 'Since we are busy transforming our world, I thought it appropriate to do a little self transformation.'

'What happens now?' asked Penny.

'Now we must be patient. We will trust that the human world will come into the light.'

'*Alchemy!*' said Penny.

'Yes,' smiled the Oracle, 'alchemy'.

'What's *alchemy?*' whispered Marty to Rufus.

'I don't know,' Rufus whispered back. 'But it doesn't sound very tasty. I'll pass.'

'Oracle, can you explain something for us?' asked Penny.

'Ruby keeps having this dream. A woman stands with her foot on a rock, looking out over a grey, stormy sea and the far horizon. Who is this woman?'

'Don't you remember?' said the Oracle quietly.

'Remember? Remember what?' answered Penny, a little confused.

'How you loved that spot.'

'*Me*? What do you mean, *me*?'

'Ruby is dreaming of *you*, Penny.'

'But I'm a cat!'

The Oracle looked at her silently. Penny thought she could see a twinkle of amusement in his eyes. Then he said: 'How do you suppose it's easy for you to speak with Ruby? And to know all those poems?'

'Didn't I learn them from Ruby?' Penny was taken aback. Her tail twitched and she quickly licked it in a flurry of irritation.

'Perhaps...' the Oracle looked up at the sky. 'Or maybe Ruby learnt them from you?'

Simone felt compelled to jump in and say something: 'What's she doing out there in the wilds?'

'She is taking balm from nature.'

'What do you mean?' Simone cocked her head.

The Oracle answered by saying:

The spray on your skin.
The roar of the waves in your ears.
The overwhelming gloom of the storm in your eyes.
The sea air in your mouth.
The salty torrent in your nostrils.

'Why is she gazing out to sea?' asked Simone.

'She is looking for that which is lost. She is looking for her "deserted garden". It can only be found in the nature.'

'How?' asked Simone.

The Oracle's final words of wisdom were these:

In the silences between the sounds of the world.
In the spaces which lie between solid objects.
Learning to meld one into another.
To dissolve the error of separation:
These all take you back into the Field of Hum.
Our awareness of the Field of Hum is lost.
It is a deserted garden.
Now it is found.

'Was that one of Ruby's poems?' asked Simone.

'No, that was mine. I know, I should have been a poet, don't you think?' replied the Oracle. 'But that is enough for today. I am rather weary. It has been such a task.'

'Why don't you come out and celebrate the new day?' asked Penny. 'Join everyone.'

'No, I'll just stay quiet in my hutch and eat my apple. Marty has strict instructions not to bring any celery. You young things go on without me.'

'I wish you would join us,' implored Simone.

The Oracle coughed, looking old and tired. 'When one thing ends another begins' he mumbled, apparently not hearing her, and hobbled off to his hutch.

'He's just pulling your leg, you know,' said Rufus. 'He's making it all up.'

'Oh Rufus, don't spoil things!' implored Marty.

Rufus pondered for a moment, then turned to Miss Davenport and locked *his* eyes on *her*, 'You look very enchanting, today, Miss Davenport.'

'*What* did you say?' she said, taken aback.

'*Enchanting*. You look very *enchanting* this morning,' he said to the boss sheep.

Miss Davenport then did something no one had ever seen: she *blushed*.

Rufus strode off to inspect the garbage as she stared after him.

'He's not such a bad little fellow. He *is* a rat after all. You *could* get used to him I suppose,' she murmured to no one in particular.

A new morning horizon greeted the animals as they left the tree and strode out across the field into the light: splashes of pink and gold reflecting in their eyes. The sound of the Hum was especially dense and enveloping this morning, as though nature was playing her orchestra.

'You were right all along,' said Penny to Simone. 'It is the end of the world, just like in your *seeing*. But the world that is ending held all the bad things. And now a new one begins with changed hearts and minds.'

Two weeks later, the Shire was abuzz with the news. *The Wingaroo Post* recorded:

Mining Company Packs its Bags

The Southern Mining Corporation, which had been granted exploration licences on many of the farms throughout this Shire, has announced it will no longer be continuing its operations here in the Shire. A spokesman for the company said there were insufficient reserves verses the cost of exploration, rendering the project unviable. Of course, for farmers in the Shire this is the best news all year. Bob Taylor, whose family has been farming here for four generations, said that the mining threat had demoralised everyone in the farming community.

"News that the explorations are now ceasing," he said, "is better than a whole season of summer rain."

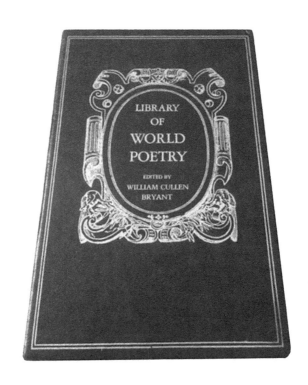

~ Finis ~

More about the Field of Hum:
www.thefieldofhum.com

Jon Gamble

Jon wrote his first novella at the age of 12. At age 15 he won the local short story competition in his home town. He studied Arts/Law at Monash University, with honours in history. He is the author of 6 non-fiction books. The Field of Hum is his first published novel, and his first work for younger readers. He lives on a little farm with his wife and daughter, and animals, in the Southern Highlands of New South Wales, Australia.

Acknowledgements

I don't think stories ever belong *entirely* to the teller. Stories come out of a collection of life experiences, people in whose company we have dwelt, other books we have read. Those experiences and people breathe life into our stories' characters, so that they may take on a life of their own. The characters in this story have certainly done that for me. They all had something very clear to say as they dictated their story to me.

Those who have directly influenced the story I now want to thank.

Dena Leighton and Anna Priest have spent many hours editing this manuscript and I am gratefully in their debt. Thank you also to Nyema Hermiston and Jo Wing, both of whose feedback has helped shape the story. I am also very grateful to Laurel Cohn and Madeline Oliver for their advice.

There were a number of young adults who reviewed the early versions of the manuscript: my daughter Rose, Susan Chen, Adelaide Poulos, Abby Miller.

My illustrator, Jennifer Black, has helped bring the characters alive.

Thank you to my wife, Nyema, and daughter, Rose, for allowing me the time and space to write: that is a true treasure.

To all those with whom I spent precious time at the Wat many years ago, you know who you are. Robbie Wesley in particular, for inspiring me to write.

Poems

First lines of each poem extract in this book, with author and title:

I mind me in the days departed
Elizabeth Barrett Browning, *The Deserted Garden*

So hush! I will give you this leaf to keep
Robert Browning, *Evelyn Hope*

The voice I hear this passing night
John Keats, *Ode to a Nightingale*

Adieu! Adieu! thy plaintive anthem fades
John Keats, *Ode to Nightingale*

The Time hath laid his mantle by
Charles of Orleans, *Spring*

I was angry with my friend
William Blake, *The Poison Tree*

And I waterd it in fears
William Blake, *The Poison Tree*

Away, away, from men and towns
Percy Shelley, *Invitation*

For now Winter's rains and ruins are over
Algernon Swinburne, *When the Hounds of Spring*

Come to these scenes of peace
William Bowles, *Come to these Scenes of Peace*

Again the violet of our early days
Ebenezer Elliot, *Spring*

Here is a gift for you
Ruby Brown, *Here is a Gift for You*

The spray on your skin
The Oracle, *The spray on Your Skin*

In the silences between the sounds of the world
The Oracle, *In the Silences Between the Sounds of the World*

Printed in Australia
AUHW011856160719
314716AU00005B/9

9 780975 247372